THE DEADLANDS
WINTER 2026

THE DEADLANDS
ISSUE 41, WINTER 2026

ISBN-13: 979-8-89116-022-4

Psychopomp.com

Publisher's Note:

For more information, contact Psychopomp: ask@psychopomp.com

This publication is a work of fiction. Names, characters, places, and incidents either are products of the authors imaginations or are used fictitiously. Any resemblance to actual persons, living or dead, events, or locales is entirely coincidental.

Publisher: Sean Markey
Editor in Chief: E. Catherine Tobler
Poetry Editor: Nicasio Andres Reed
Social Media: Felicia Martínez
Art Director: inkshark
Nonfiction Editor: David Gilmore
Necromancer at Large: Amanda Downum
Copy Editor: Laura Blackwell
Copy Editor: Annika Barranti Klein
Designer: Christine M. Scott
Cover: *Silver Island* by Carly A-F

The Deadlands is distributed quarterly by:
    Psychopomp
    PO Box 36
    Woodbury, VT 05681

Subscriptions can be purchased at weightlessbooks.com. Individual issues can be obtained by joining our Patreon (with many deadly perks).

Join here: thedeadlands.com/patreon

WINTER 2026

GUEST FICTION EDITOR:

VAJRA CHANDRASEKERA

PSYCHOPOMP

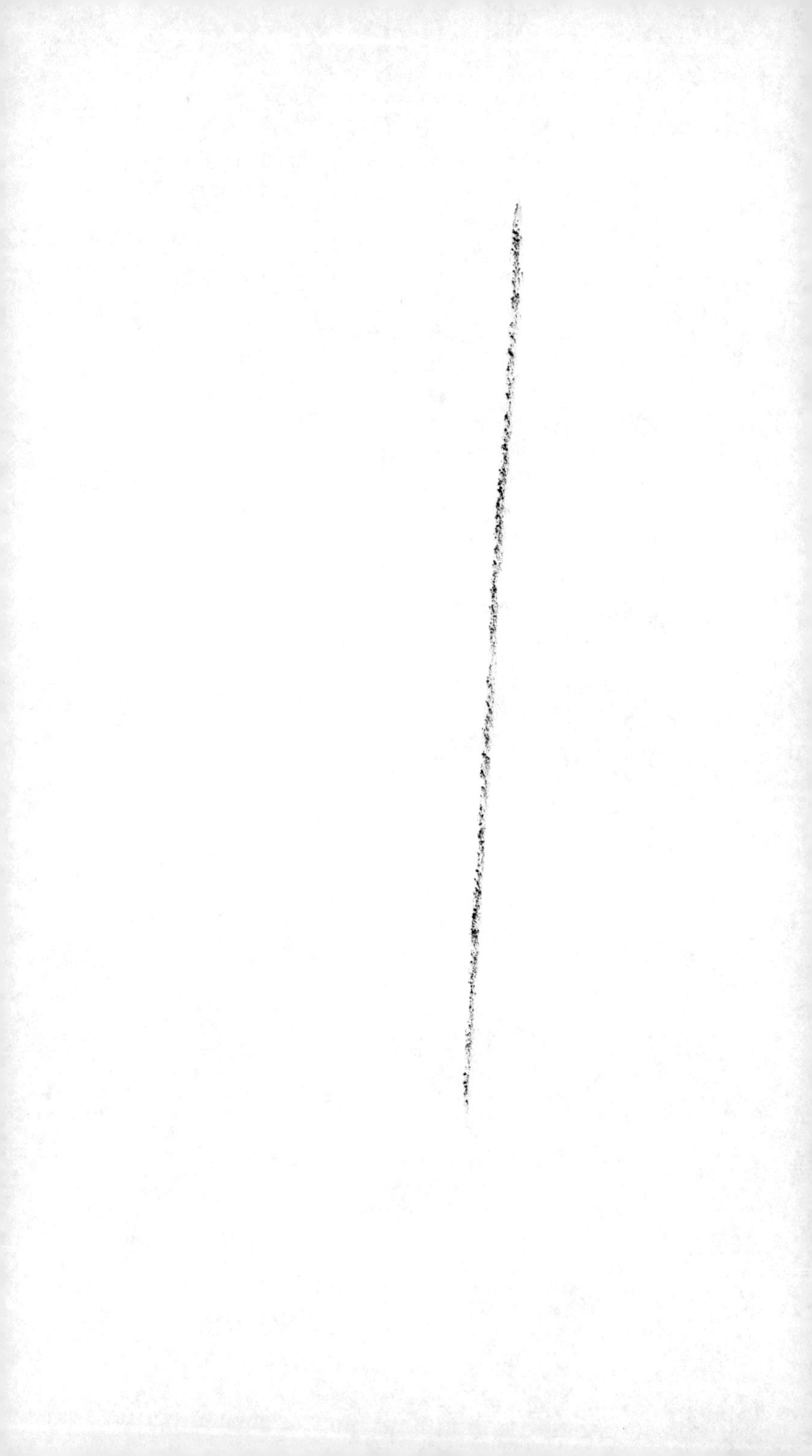

TABLE OF CONTENTS

TABLE OF CONTENTS

Poetry

BARK!

Charlotte Suttee

awoken!
  by the opening blow
of a shut thing—
    the latch!
of a short-sighted dog
              bark!
he says
   it is night!

the white moon rolls
   ballpoint on black sky
a word too long to be read by any less
   than the great conjoined eye
of our generation (lost mulling
     over lawns—
              bark!
   the near-blind dog hinges
back!
   he says
back to that
   made up childhood
back!
   to the spelling books
wide barn doors and hay
   when we all
took after the lean trees
   not a death in you
or me

Fiction

THE SKULL OF FRANCISCO XALBEC

Alan M. Fisher

EVERY TIME I died, I received another coin to place in the skull of Francisco Xalbec. The skull was ornate, layered in gold with silver rimming the eye sockets, in which sat multifaceted black gems. Whenever I dropped another coin in the skull, it reflected a thousandfold in those dark eyes, as did the face that I knew was mine yet couldn't recognize. The seam down the center of the skull, which should have been fused, had a small opening, a slit just wide enough to take the coins. I'd dropped hundreds, maybe thousands, of coins into the skull of Francisco Xalbec, and I still wasn't sure how full it was, but I knew with profound certainty that I had to fill it.

To fill it I had to die, for each death brought me a coin to place in the skull of Francisco Xalbec. Despite what you might think, it is not always easy to die. From time to time I would try to bash my brains out on the stone walls of the room in which the skull of Francisco Xalbec sat, but instead of an eternal blackness and a new coin coldly resting in my palm, I would merely wake minutes or hours later, in pain and hair matted with blood. So I must venture out of my room and into the labyrinth, a maze of stone corridors and stairwells and doorways, always hunting a death. Sometimes finding a death was simple, a yawning chasm of darkness in which I could plunge, to die and awaken with a new coin. Sometimes a death was hard, a long flight of rough stairs that I had to work up the courage to throw myself down, headfirst, hoping for a death and not mere agony.

Sometimes in the labyrinth I would find another person, claiming that they were looking for a death so they could get a coin, but not a coin to place in the skull of Francisco Xalbec.

They claimed their skulls had other names—Marsha Drake, or Pieter van Dorn, or Ayisha Alwan—and they all lied. There was only the skull of Francisco Xalbec. I would try to goad them into killing me, while they tried to goad me into killing them, until finally we would fight, two people trying to kill themselves at the hands of the other.

Sometimes a death found me, a raven-haired woman who hunted me, smashed in my skull with a rock, shot me with an arrow, or slit my throat with an obsidian blade, and I would die and awaken again with a cold coin to place in the skull of Francisco Xalbec. I feared her.

I think I loved her.

This time, I found some rope and strangled myself, rough fiber cutting blood from my neck. Awakening on the ground with a cold coin in my hand. The coin, like all the coins, was forged from fragments, the wing of an eagle, part of a face, a zero. My fingers knew these fragments, I had callouses from them, I remembered piecing them together into coins for the skull of Francisco Xalbec. Had I once shorn them against my ruins, or was I remembering someone else's words? It didn't matter, what was in my past was past. What mattered is that I placed the coin in the skull of Francisco Xalbec and, as I had done every time before, I tried to pick it up. Every time the skull had not moved, but this time it did, and I lifted the skull of Francisco Xalbec and it was heavy with coins. I shifted it from side to side, but it was so full of my death coins that nothing rattled. I hefted it before me and the skull of Francisco Xalbec, in a voice made of shifting coins, told me where to go, how to navigate the labyrinth, and I obeyed.

I do not know how long we walked, the skull of Francisco Xalbec and I, through the labyrinth, past its many twists and turns, past its pits and stairs, past the other seekers of death who looked on me with awe, for I, and I alone, was walking with my skull. We came to a wooden door which swung open for us.

My killer sat on the edge of a well in a round room. "Finally, you're back," she said. "Perhaps this is the one."

"You killed me," I replied, more weary than fearful, and she nodded.

"You were taking too long," she said with a smile.

"I know. I'm sorry. Where do you want the skull of Francisco Xalbec?" She motioned to the well. I looked in and it was nearly full of golden skulls with silver-rimmed eye sockets filled with dark multifaceted gems. I placed the skull of Francisco Xalbec on the top of the pile of what I realized were skulls of Francisco Xalbec. She moved close to the edge, and anticipation radiated from her.

With a grinding noise, the skulls began to drain away. The room filled with the thunder of skulls rolling against each other as they fell, the shifting of an eternity of coins ringing like bells. She leapt with joy. "Oh, Francisco, that was the last one," she shouted. She hugged me and kissed me on the lips. "I have to go." She climbed into the well and began to sink as the skulls rattled away into the dark. "Good luck," she called. "May your time go faster!"

And she was gone. I looked over the rim of the well and saw nothing but deep darkness. Silence fell over the room. I looked into the darkness as if it might grant enlightenment, and started when the door opened. A man was standing there, holding a golden skull with silver-rimmed eye sockets filled with dark multifaceted gems. "Hello," he said hesitantly, "where do you want the skull of Magnus Carboni?" I memorized his face, so I would know it when I went hunting, and motioned toward the well. He tossed the skull of Magnus Carboni into its dark depths, and I heard the coins within it shifting as it fell.

Fiction

THE SELF-MADE WOMEN'S CIRCLE

Marisca Pichette

TODAY we are taking my daughter apart.

She knows. Some of her friends at school have already changed, returning from the weekend with lopsided pigtails and too-big hands. She hasn't spoken to me about it, but I know she will have ideas of how she wants to be remade. We will do our best to honor her wishes.

At 7:00 a.m., I patch myself together in the mirror. Lips stitched to face, bones cleaned and screwed in place. Hair brushed and hooked, hands washed and put together again. Over everything I fold mottled skin, inherited from women whose names have long since vanished into obscurity.

My mother's hooks are silver, delicate, and polished to perfection. Nine in all, they clutter my jewelry box, mingling with rings and bracelets she never wears anymore.

The first time I put them on, lined up along my scalp—pale in the bathroom mirror under unforgiving fluorescent light—they clashed with my gold hoops. Silver has always been her color.

My sister's hooks are steel: cold and fierce. The five I traded connect fingers to my right hand. In the winter, they grow so cold they burn.

When my grandmother died, her hooks scattered through the family like pollen in spring. I got three, greened copper that stains the skin stretched over my breasts. Looking at myself in the mirror, I wonder who donated the hooks that held her together. The women in my family have no last names, and first names are common as graves. Reaching back, I can only brush the last three generations before lined faces fade into hearsay. Emma, Mary, Justine. Beatrice and Sarah, Annette and Lee. Nicknames deepen the mystery, wipe our fullness out until everyone I know is partial, shortened for others' ease.

To be female is to be a footnote. I am an assemblage—my hair fastened in place, a gift from an aunt who decided one morning not to rise. My eyes are mismatched. When my mother helped me press them into my sockets, she whispered their stories to me. Left: brown, a daughter who died. Right: cataracted green, recovered from a great-grandmother unmade a week before my time. I owe her also the fingers of my left hand, brittle and scarred. Their hooks were reforged from her wedding ring.

I add my jewelry: gold rings to match some hooks and clash with others. As a finishing touch, I put on makeup, smoothing out the borders between bodies. Today is special, after all.

Complete as I can be, I leave the bathroom on uneven feet. I pause by my daughter's bedroom. She's sleeping still. Leaving her to rest as much as possible, I prepare the house for company. I clear the kitchen table and start coffee in the pot. I make fresh ice in the tray and swipe the cobwebs from the ceiling corners. As I sterilize knives in the sink, women arrive.

Mothers, sisters, daughters. Aunts, cousins, grandmothers. I am related to all in the way that all insects share the fear of being crushed. Pieces of them occupy pieces of me—and every scrap remembers its whole.

Low voices mingle in the kitchen as hooked-together hands fold clothes and roll up sleeves. We have no fathers, no brothers. They are as alien to us as we are to them, and we can't blame them for shying away from this gathering. Because when is the last time you heard about a man prized apart, dissected to preserve the choicest cuts? What man would recycle wrinkled skin to hide vulnerable youth, donning a mask to pretend at expiration?

My mother takes my hand in hers while the coffee burbles behind us. Some of our fingers match. "How is she?"

I check the clock on the wall, listing towards nine. "She'll be awake soon."

"Is she scared?" my grandmother asks. "Does she know what to expect?"

"I do."

We turn to see my daughter standing in the doorway, her hair a mess around her face. Her eyes are the same, her skin clear. We don't look much alike at all.

The assembled women bow to her, hooks rattling in concert. Taking her hands, we lead her to the kitchen chair. She climbs up onto the waiting table without hesitation. The air is thick with the smell of coffee and disinfectant. I step forward, cupping my daughter's face in my fractured hand.

"You can choose your first piece," I say. "What would you like?"

She looks from me to her grandmother, her aunt, her cousin. Biting her lip, she points.

"Your hands," she says to my great-aunt. "They look strong."

My great-aunt nods and unhooks her hands with the help of her own daughter. I pick up the knife.

My little girl doesn't scream as I cut her hands away to trade. She doesn't cry when we drive hooks into her wrists. She says nothing as we barter her body, dividing her skin and hair between us, integrating our likenesses until she is just as mottled as me.

When we have finished, the table stained red and my hands stiff from cutting, the coffee is burned in the pot. No matter; it all tastes the same to hand-me-down tongues.

We retire to the living room with cups and saucers. My daughter shuns assistance, walking alone on mismatched feet. I look at her, and I see my scars.

I want to say I'm sorry. I want to scream, put her back the way she was—but she's stronger now. Now her chances might be better.

We sit in a circle, sipping in silence, save for the myriad clinking of metal hooks.

IN WHICH ORPHEUS IS A HMONG DAUGHTER

Phoua Lee

a marketplace for souls trading in paper money
for an item from their loved ones.
            something small
                 something unnoticed.
        bells   clinking
the man with wheat skin
cataract eyes with crow's feet
black trousers torn raw at the hems
trades in his last crumpled joss bill
for one of his daughter's pens, still warm with
life from her hand. jostled by the milling crowd,
his branch-gnarled fingers quiver. two strings
of fate—
one attached   to his wrist,
the other   to the pen.
both ordained   to part ways.
it falls on the ground. neither find
their way back to each other.

a child worms through the huddle,
half his face ripened pink in delight, the other
half a deformed tragedy from an indiscriminate fire.
blade in his left fist, slices the patched pocket of
an unsuspecting woman mulling over honey melons.
a single coin fills the basin of his hand. disappointed,
he kicks up dust, slouches away, hands in his pockets,
laden with cut holes. not by his own design.

the stall owner's hawk eyes shoot   air-thin   needles

down Gao-Jer's spine. "you're not supposed to be here"
is a speculation, but when uttered from the lips
of the dead, morphs into a warning for which
there is no refutation. joss paper for a pair
of hemp shoes shuts him up,
asks her if she'd like to buy shoe cleaner solution
for an extra fee. they have that down here?
yeah, made from the drool of hungry ghosts.
proceeds go towards their finances for food,
or if they're lucky, a pair of hemp shoes. she rejects
the offer. he suggests holding the shoes close to
her chest. two possibilities:

the shoes rip
                                or she rips,
both torn by desirous ghosts.

                                twelve great mountains span
the thunder-soot sky, smoldered with whaleback
clouds. a mother's love is enough to traverse
all mountains, but a daughter's love is enough
to follow after them. Gao-Jer is one with the
soldiering ghost crowd, edging towards the
first mountain. a little girl beside her asks how
she died. *grief,* she responds. not the truth but as close
as she'll get. the wind picks up, and Gao-Jer offers
the girl her jacket. she's moved to tears. "since i
came here the cold has followed me." from this,
Gao-Jer knows how she died. mov nplaum wrapped
in banana leaves falls in Gao-Jer's hands
from the grace of the little girl's. "the second mountain
is a pit of gluttony." don't be eaten and don't eat
others. the first is a death of the soul. the latter is
a curse. all perpetrators are condemned to being
feasted upon forever on the mountain. Gao-Jer pinches the
hemp shoes to her chest and recites her mother's name.

            second mountain offers no seconds
for those who are hungry. a frothing cauldron boils
above a fire pit. scent of stinging spring onions and
bittersweet oyster sauce hangs
           in
               the
                   air,
but the underlying whiff of innocent flesh forms
a resistance in the passing ghosts, all determined to
prove themselves stronger than their hunger.
mov nplaum in her pocket warms her thigh and
speaks to her craving. a mother's love is enough to
feed her children, but a daughter's love
feeds the mother. a man who crawls on four limbs
approaches her after he's done feeding on carrion.
"your mother left this for you—one week ago—knew
you'd probably come. poor her, she must be so hungry.
—i can't eat them. mortal food poisons me."
spindle-like fingers caress a cloth-covered package
—her mother's embroidery. she unravels its content:
succulent, scarlet-shelled rambutans bursting with the
syrup of life. one bite and juices drip down her chin
accompanied by tears of joy or yearning, or *missing*—
she doesn't know. the man catches a glimpse of her
mother's hemp shoes, gnashes at her arm with
razor teeth. she flings him away and escapes.

                third, fourth, fifth mountain.
Dab Ntxwj Nyug's heavenly cattle dot the reed-grass plains,
stare at her with beaded eyes like tapioca pearls.
one of them cries, an animal yet to separate
from the residuals of their human life

Gao-Jer is the same.

sixth mountain is a rolling mass of hairy
caterpillars. a single pierce in the foot is a pierce in the

spirit heart for a string of lifetimes. at the foot,
a woman waits in the skirt of fog. cataract eyes with
crow's feet, blindly roving to and fro. back hunched,
fingers knotted at the joints as she kneels to feel at
the sparse grass beneath her bare-veined feet. Gao-Jer
places a single, unshelled rambutan in her withered palm—
an offering, almost, but no less than a
       hello   and
         nice to meet you again.
this is one of mother's many souls, stripped of its eyesight.

i'm sorry i'm late
i'm sorry we have to meet under these circumstances.

her mother writes code in her palm for forgiveness,
traces her features with her fingers like this is her
final act of rebellion, remembering her past before
she severs their connection forever, as she's supposed to.
the hemp shoes are a memento of Gao-Jer's journey,
surprisingly intact, and she marvels at what it means
to take something delicate and hold it that gently without
crushing it alive. she becomes a kneeling sentinel, fits
the hemp shoes on her mother's feet, and wishes them
to magically disappear so she would have no reason
to leave. she yearns for tus qeej to sing her
mother a path back, but if she doesn't want a way back,
Gao-Jer—with these shoes—will give her a
                 way
                   forward.

     she doesn't know this, but Gao-Jer has
stuffed the mov nplaum in her mother's pocket.

        her mother smiles.
body wrapped up in fog, she wafts away,
the edges of her ghostly silhouette tragically soft

like any dandelion waiting to be blown away.

the rambutan is back in Gao-Jer's hand,
and this time she crushes it.

Fiction

ON THE ANTHOLOGY ENTITLED "FRAMES OF COLOUR AND UN-COLOUR"

Dmitri Akers

I WRITE this to you now, under appreciable mental malady. Forgive me. My mind and heart, and my vocabulary with them, err. The film you wanted me to develop—it is done. But the latter half of the roll was tainted by light. From red glares to pallid frames of exposure, like blood pouring into the whiteness of hell. Hell must be pale. I know now.

But what remains visible in the developed film is awful. Things a man should not see. You are a sick man for photographing them. I send these photos on a developed reel; you will have to scan them yourself; I cannot do it. I hate the technology that allows scanning, printing, and higher definitions. Now, I have sent them in this tube that you have undoubtedly opened, if you have opened this at all. I send you a complementary description of each photograph, since your blind brother cannot see; you can explain them to him, so he does not miss out.

Regards,
The Luddite.

The Anthology

Find twenty-four photos, most of which are tainted, or wholly erased.

I: The first photo is not crisp. Too shadowy, underexposed, the camera shakes; the aperture cannot catch the field's swaying hemlocks. A blue of outlines and shapes, a crude blending of light and dark. There is no contrast between light and shadow, only a deeper blue of melancholy. Elysian Fields in the shade of a poet's ink, before the poet writes a haiku upon the gates of death.

II: A wide shot. Inside, the field is now in focus. I see the hemlocks for once, in their pure blooms of deathly white, as buds rustle by the side (slightly blurred). Above lingers the cloudless sky of pale (almost whitish) blue. It is the same blue as a calm sea on a flat coast of unstirred sand. Below, the waves of flowers are visible as far as possible, until graininess and shadows consume the latter half of the field. By the far right corner, an elm grows, but it is mostly a shadow that leans inland. The sun must be on the other side, to the right, to the west. I guess it is midafternoon.

III: A closer shot of the elm. From the same direction as before, only much closer. It is in the centre of the picture. An elm, but it fits inside a box within the frame! Its lower branches droop along the side, as higher branches climb towards the sun. Tones of greens, browns, emeralds, blacks, and the purplish of aubergines in some corners. The western leaves, illumined by sun, turn almost gold; the eastern leaves, shrouded in darkness, turn blacker than pitch into the invisibility of pitch. The elm stands, little etchings along its bark-armour; riverine trenches scrape across its flesh, showing its scars from the passage of time's flow.

IV: Close to a single leaf of the elm, rimed with some white, sticky substance; its serrated edges of jade are softened. They are of an off hue. And they curl inward, and bits slough off here and there, as steel may be softened by acid. Although grainy, I see the damaged leaf in its totality; the foreground can only hold this leaf, despite its dying away. It sits on top of raging waters, that swell of blurriness in the background; it looks to be the grass beneath the tree, construed as mayhem.

V: A close shot of the elm's hole. A large hole; I guess it could fit a head, or two heads. It looks hungry. Like a leech's sucker. The hollow of the tree is dark, as dark as the inmost depth of hell; lips of grooved bark line the edge of the hole. They look distended, like fat, pregnant eels slithering over another. Cords of blubber coiling around the hole. The hole is a window into hell, I think.

VI: Inside the blackness of a well, I see some eyes glow. They are blue. Blue as lotuses, blue as the Aegean, blue as sapphires. They twinkle inside that pitch darkness; until, it seems, the whole photo is out of focus, if not for the eyes. The cameraman (is he you?) can see the eyes; he must have. For he now points his camera right at the set of eyes, and I only see the two blue dots, hovering almost, or revolving around another, inside the bleak abyss inside the elm's mouth.

VII: It emerges. The pair of eyes, that is. They are compound eyes, upon a strange face. It is an insect's. Likely a scarab, or a locust. I do not know. The front portion of the bug is visible. Other than that, it has the outline of the topmost portion of a carapace. The armour of a centurion. Does this thing have wings? It is brown, mostly ovoid from the front, with a pair of eyes that contains more and more pairs of eyes, *ad infinitum.* They glow. They glow. Cerulean seas. Banshees.

VIII: The whole body of the insect. It sits along the edge of the elm's mouth, descending down the trunk. Through grains and spots, I still see the intricate details along the back of the bug's armour. It has a line going down it, a black line, that bleeds out into peacock patterns: rainbow eyes, flames of every hue, layers of colour over another, like a colourful slick of oil in water, or a decadent cocktail of various painted densities. It is a scarab, or beetle-like in design. I think it is a coleopteran, if it is indeed a living specimen of insect, and not a spirit from the hellish void it emerged from. The scarab has a black mark on its back, barely visible if not studied for; it is an hourglass shape, amidst the spectral lights.

IX: More and more bugs. In this mid-shot, a few paces back from before, the elm is less in focus, and the sward around it is blurred into greenish hazes and spectral haunts of evergreen. Tendril-vines descend as fallen leaves blur into singular ropy masses of blurriness. But the bugs come. More and more. They are in the centre of the frame; if I sliced the photograph in nine boxes, it would be in the middle of them. A rule of thirds. But the bugs come. More and more. They are spilling out from the void. In focus, they look like teardrops of rainbow colours, and blue eyes sparkling in the colour of it.

X: The sun shines on them, as they spill out in their multitudes. Dozens of dozens, hundreds of hundreds, as their shiny backs are conglomerating into one immense kaleidoscope. Waves and waves. Crashing seas of every hue of paint. But the wings come, buzzing; they look like streaks of brown or grey or ash. They contrast no colour, but fill the vibrancy with specks of dullness. The hollowness of the black mouth is gone. I see only flying scarabs and light, and colours of colours, bouncing off another, making more colours!

XI: A spot of blood lines the edge of the photo: the top, right corner. Blood? I do not know. But they come. More and more in number. Until there is no way to quantify anything that is in such quantity. It is featureless, unknowable, ever-shifting. The scourge, the bugs, the limitless. Scarabs flying, screeching almost, from within the photograph. Gold liquid pouring into the greenest jade, as bloody rubies mix with the bluest essence of lotus's intoxicating wine. Velvet and silk intermix with the darkest amethyst; sparkles of silver dot the photograph, making the grains of colourless nothingness almost invisible. Bugs. Bugs. They are coming, until too much colour gives way to lack of definition, lack of contrast, lack of vibrancy.

XII: Bloody drops of see-through light. They glimmer along the edges, into some of the corners, along the outermost flat dimensions (X, Y) of the photograph. If there is a Z dimension, the light leaks dance in that space: red ghosts of vengeance. The scene is that of insectoid hell; wings pour out of opened carapaces, which are grooved and spotted with grains of sand, amidst a maelstrom of half-formed things that flow from corporeal into incorporeal, from whole into parts (and back again), as well as the chimeric amalgamation of solids, liquids, gases, and suspended particles. Scarabs fly, their wretched probosces set to suck, their damned compound eyes are leering even from the prison of this frozen image. Space and time hold still; the awakening furies, those tides of rapture, are stirring. Death is upon us.

XIII: Underneath the halos of dreaded reds and beams of scarlet, I see the hordes of bugs swarm towards the camera. Although the shot is still, I can see a mere finger begin to poke its way in the field of view; the cameraman is anxious; he knows, I think you know he knows, that he is about to die. Where did you find this camera again? I have not ventured outside since the great cataclysm, and I hope you do not bring the deathly scourge on my doorstep with this omen. Seas of a murrain, hosts of pestilence! Their awful, crude shapes are brimming across the photograph, in hues of darkness and drabness, taking away the colour of the fields—the white hemlocks, the green stems, the elm's leaves, the emeraldine sward!

XIV: Bloody bands, myriads of furious spirits, the Satanic host of vermilion and orange and gold. They dance on top of the rest of it. A phantasmagoria. Within, or beneath them, I see the scarabs' horrible eyes glowing in shades of blues or azures. Revenant blues. For they are now covered over with reds, making them purplish. Purplish like lavender in winter, rusting away into off, pale hues of purple. Until pinks and other derivatives of pure red begin to take hold.

XV: Under a river of bloody surge, a flood of ichor, a deluge of death, I see the scarabs moving and moving quicker; their shapes are not shapes. They are morphing into one single shape. As an urn may only have its whole form to make it an urn, the scarabs are one thing. They are not their parts, their sectioned-off curves, their rudimentary atoms. The whole photo is the whole horde of wings and glowing eyes; it looks more like a poorly shot constellation in the night, with a low enough exposure of light, to contain some of the stars. Sparkling votive candles, beneath the blood; purples, reds, but more reds than anything. An endless sea of faceless creatures, that forms its own face, the face of decomposition. The god of decay is smiling.

XVI: A ghostly white edge glows along the eastern side. A spot of milk? Something poured onto the top of this photo? No. It is light pollution. A leak. Within that faceless rabble host of insects, I see the definition of no single thing; only the pseudo-shapes, that seem half-tears and half-leaves, fall across most of the frame. Their motion is obvious, since the aperture and shutter speed are not set for their velocity and acceleration. Only some of the wings are frozen in time, but they are also poorly blended into the rest of the scenery; hues of black, brown, silver, white, and smatterings of purplish fill the majority of the photo. I see, inside the hollow, two distinct dots of gold. They look like eyes. Or the reflections that eyes tend to make, inside the reflections of mirrors, or cameras. Blood-reds warp the usual opacity of the photo, creating translucent and dancing eidolons (coloured like lifeblood); they dance in refractive glory, dancing for the bloodshed of Ilion.

XVII: By the edges, the sanguine dun becomes, measure by measure, white as a sheet. The redness is dying away into a cadaver's pale and colourless flesh; drained of blood, the photo begins to look almost stark. The raving mad things, whatever they are, drain away in their multitudes, until I see the hollow again. Draining the world of locusts, the hollowed maw of the elm is filled. He once again eats up what he spewed: the locusts, which are still there, flying across half the frame. But, on the eastern side of the frame, sunlight-beams glitter along the leaves, making them yellow and gold, as red taint gives way to the white wall that destroys most of the photo. Whiteness makes annihilation. And yet, the warring insects still bang their proverbial shields and fly into the fray of the foreground …. If not for the hollowed elm's sucking hole.

XVIII: Most of the photo is erased, except for the faint shadow of a screaming mouth in the top left corner, which brims with the life of death. Buzzing, screeching horrors, I can hear them! Their wings are blurred, their shapes are amorphous, out of focus, and yet I hear them! I hear them from beyond! The screech and whine of their songs, with the monotonous blowing clarion of the abyss. I hear it! I hear it! The sounds of cicadas, the choir of scarabs, the drone of moth wings, the hum of a million wasps, the single tone of countless locusts flying over the Nile! My ears are bleeding at the immensity of these booming, crashing waves, waves over waves, ply over ply, of endless, deafening din!

XIX: Blank, white, deathly white, carte blanche. Sea-foam.

XX: White as hemlock's flowers inside Elysium. I see nothing but whiteness's infinity of colourlessness.

XXI: White as the dust of cremations; powders of lead; sugarcane beetles' chitin.

XXII: White ash, white with the hues of purgatory, white like shit turns white, white like a scarab beetle covered in white shit.

XXIII: Asphodel, painted over with the purest paint. Seraphim wings' feathers. The moon's stunning whiteness in a pitch-black night, but there is no darkness here to speak of, except the darkness where the purest band of light occupies.

XXIV: Hell is a sea of pallid hemlock milk. Everything is quiet.

Nonfiction

BIBLE VERSES FOR THE DYING AND THE HEATHEN

Robin Wheeler

MY PARENTS' home was never mine. They bought the three-acre plot of farmland with the eighty-year-old Queen Anne farmhouse when I was almost sixteen. When they tore out the rotting chicken coop that summer and unearthed a tattered white dress, my mom concocted a story that it belonged to the original owners' daughter. Perhaps they buried it under the chicken shit when she disgraced the family in a way that rendered a white dress unnecessary. And maybe her spirit lived in the charred rafters of the attic that opened into my bedroom.

My paternal grandmother grew up three blocks away. The first time she saw a fire truck, it was extinguishing a fire at the house my parents would buy in 1988.

The house my maternal grandparents would eventually buy across the road from my parents' home wouldn't be built until the 1950s. A clan that couldn't bear to be even a mile apart. I lived three hours away, a deserter.

But when my maternal granny was in hospice care in her home, I returned with no plan to go home until I saw her off to the grave. No matter how foreign the house felt, or how displaced I was.

To my nose, the old farmhouse held both the smells of my childhood and of aging, that combination of mothballs and menthol that I doubt anyone else noticed. I never knew my mom to use mothballs, but the odor was unmistakable in its warning of impending decay.

Menthol, I understood. It was the scent of muscle knots and splintered joints. The longer I was at their house, with its steep back porch steps and the staircase to my bedroom, the walk through the grass to and from the deathbed across the road, the more I felt every movement below the inner dimple of my right knee, requiring the numbing stink of ointments and creams.

But outside the house, tangles and trellises of flowers engulfed the patio, mingling with the earthy hay, the summer heat, and manure from the horses. Between the house and the pasture, floral overgrowth buried the stepping stones. They led to the cavernous metal garage where my dad sold horse tack and guns surrounded by the rough-hewn leather and sweat-soaked saddle blankets, a comforting haze for the visitors who stopped to see Granny and then wandered over to visit my parents on the slab of concrete outside the garage.

July heat usually topped triple digits, with the air a thick, milky stew. But that July it abated, the temperature lingering in the low 80s, prompting distant relatives from out of town to come say goodbye. Such a pretty day for a drive. Let's go say goodbye. It didn't occur to anyone to wheel Granny Viv's hospital bed to the deck of the house to enjoy the weather that was making her blackberries a bumper crop. And she never would have asked, already mortified at putting anyone out, being so much trouble.

She knew her time was ending. Just days, but she didn't feel the strum of pain or the numbness of morphine. She just felt tired. And worried—the feeling that dictated her life. Confident she'd meet her savior, she didn't worry about death. She worried instead about if the blackberries had been picked yesterday. She worried about where Grandpa Charlie would go if he couldn't stay in the house without her. She worried about whether all her guests on the deck needed iced tea refills, or cold cans of pop.

She felt the joy of holding her six-month-old great-grandson, the supple skin of each baby toe in her dry-leaf fingers. These little piggies.

She worried that he and his brother would be teased for having two moms, but that's the way of the world.

She worried the family would splinter and split; she told me to stick by my cousins, knowing that she was the binding agent among these disparate people. Her two children spoke to each other only when necessary, their animosity disguised for her benefit, but she knew how they were, fighting over petty jealousies their whole lives. As for my two cousins, I was close to one. The other rarely spoke to me. But that's just the way of the men. Even the young ones.

As my first week in my parents' house wound down, my father also didn't have many words for me, other than terse ones regarding the lateness of my sleeping, my messiness when I left anything in the living room, and the incorrectness of pretty much everything I said. He, my mom, and I went for a ride one afternoon, taking in the long stretches of prairie where my grandfather was born and raised. Only the church remained. A few days before, Dad and I had flipped through a history book about the county, and he gladly pointed out the places where our family once belonged. But in the days that followed, he'd grown tired of my company and wanted none of my commentary or questions.

Back in town I asked for a stop at the Mexican ice cream shop for a mangonada. The frosty plastic cup brimmed with layers of bright, lime-soured mango and streaks of red chili and the chamoy sauce that dripped down the inside. He looked at me as I sucked and gnawed on the tamarind straw, and I knew he thought I was showing off, being intentionally weird just to embarrass him. I decided to pack and leave that night, knowing what was coming if I didn't.

During a family trip to Colorado when I was twenty-three, my father drove up a mountain while screaming all my faults to me. I was too lazy and too ambitious to have time for anything but work. Slutty and snobbish, too damn smart for my own good, and so incredibly stupid.

At first, I wailed and screamed at his accusations, trying to argue, confused at how the path kept changing. It took hours for me to realize there was nothing to argue. He was contradicting himself, so at least half of what he accused me of being had to be wrong. While I couldn't calm the hiccupping sobs, I was able to engage my voice and reply, "You're right. You're absolutely right," to each couplet that frothed from his mouth with the acrid coffee breath and yellow, gapped teeth where the spittle flew out.

"You're right. You're absolutely right," I said after every declaration of my shittiness until I fell prone across the back seat, exhausted, unblinking, floating above the roof of their Ford Bronco and the fray within, one of the clouds that once drifted overhead, then became a skirt of fog below us as we gained altitude, unbothered when we drove through it even though common sense would say the Bronco should erupt each cloud into a storm.

At the top of the mountain, I remained prone in the back seat. Of my nine relatives in our mountain caravan, only Granny came to me. A bottle of cool water, a red apple, a cold washcloth she'd dunked in the melted ice in the cooler to rest over my swollen eyes, and the admission no one else in the family dared make: that she loved me.

That night, as I lay on the couch, tears leaking from my eyes when they were available, she repeated her action: a water, an apple, a cloth, an "I love you" while the clatter of dominoes and laughter peeled from the dining room.

Who would bring my child apples and water, compresses and love, if I ripped out her soul like I had come so close to doing when I defaulted to the anger I inherited from my father? Granny was the only person capable of feeling and showing that level of forgiveness for someone's unbearable humanity. I tried to exhibit my version of maternal love, but we were sleepwalking through our new grief, waking just long enough to get a glimpse of the pleasure of being alive before remembering our reality. We ate tacos in a hotel bed. That was all I knew to do. No coolness, no hydration. Just fiery, toothsome meat dripping red chili sauce.

I didn't leave that night, as the hospice nurse told us the end was near. For the first time, Granny Viv had spent the day fully encased in a blanket of morphine, her words a jumble, making sense only when she told my cousin's girlfriend to go get the fried chicken, put it on the table, and call everyone to dinner. There was no fried chicken. She'd fried her last chicken two days before she had the appointment with the cancer diagnosis. But it was important for the newest adult woman in the family to know how to serve the chicken properly.

Once the daily visitors realized there wasn't much left of Granny, they cleared out and, with no one waiting for a turn with her, I sat by her side as she mumbled at me. Unable to understand anything she said, I held her bloated hand with her familiar crooked arthritic fingers, my brain scrambling for something to say. Words of comfort, of love, anything, but it all seemed trite and futile. The idea of just telling her how much I loved her didn't even cross my mind.

Instead, I pulled my phone from my pocket and googled "Bible verses for the dying." I had no clue where to begin when it came to Christian territory, and she knew that, but in these late moments I opted to fake it.

"Jesus said to her, 'I am the resurrection and the life. Whoever believes in me, though he die, yet shall he live, and everyone who lives and believes in me shall never die. Do you believe this?'"

I did not believe this. I didn't believe anything. I hoped that maybe there was something else, something other than the follies on this ball of dirt and fire.

She believed it, had told me to make sure I believed it so she could see me again. I could pretend and hope.

She moaned.

'He will wipe away every tear from their eyes, and death shall be no more, neither shall there be mourning, nor crying, nor pain anymore, for the former things have passed away.'

Her eyes pleaded, probably in pain's delirium. Or because she knew I wasn't reading with conviction.

Granny Viv was the third dead person I ever saw, and the first who wasn't neatly tucked into a casket with a faceful of makeup over the bulge of taut, embalmed skin. She'd been gone less than five minutes when I arrived, an hour after I had returned to my parents' house. I ran through the ruts of their yard and the street after getting the call that she was on her way. If I hadn't taken the time to change out of my pajamas, I would have been there when she stretched her arm to the ceiling, locked eyes with Grandpa Charlie, and died.

When I arrived, my father met me in the driveway, shaking his head. All that was left to do was make the coffee and wait for the undertaker.

Even Grandpa eventually left her side, sat in his chair, took out his calendar and wrote "Viv" in the square for July 25. Her calico cat dozed at her feet, where stagnant blood was beginning to pool under her fragile skin, hidden by a faded Little Mermaid sheet. Her eyes closed, but her jaw slacked open, its hinge succumbing to gravity.

She'd been healthy for a ninety-two-year-old until the fast-growing tumor came. Four months prior, she'd been so healthy she'd gotten a new hip. Thousands of dollars of titanium soon to be buried in the ground, barely used.

How to grieve someone who makes it to 92, mostly healthy, whose fatal suffering was limited to a single day that required morphine? That year the average American lifespan rose to 78.7 years. At 92.45 years, we had a bonus of 13.75 years with her, every day a miracle. My grief was selfish, a wallow, because I'd never eat myself sick on her party mix at Christmas again, or reap her praise when I replicated her chicken and dumplings recipe. I loved her. I would miss her. Couldn't imagine the world without her. But we had almost fourteen years of pure, beautiful luck. How could I grieve when so many people aren't afforded such a bounty?

Instead of grieving, I played with my cousin's babies so she could grieve. Talked to Grandpa, turned the blackberries into cobblers, bought succulents at the farmer's market for my mother. I knew the time of day based on when reruns of *Friends* were on, flirted with the idea of sleep, made my choices from Granny's costume jewelry.

Not that this state of anti-grief did me or anyone any good when I returned home. I was present—going through the motions at work, preparing CJ for the new school year—but feeling like a foreigner in my own body. Like my blood had gone stagnant, too.

MUSHABOOM

Jeremy Morris

THE RIVER went nowhere. A fishing port at one end. Tendrils that snaked up to the highlands at the other. The coastline looked like a cup of spilt tea. As the road curled down to the provincial park, the asphalt was more of a suggestion than the definite article. He drove fast. Her hair blew across her face. She hadn't said a word in miles.

He complained about the chip wagon. More as banter than as true grievance.

"What did you expect from a place called *Gazoo's*?" she said.

"They only took cash," he said. "You going to barter with some cod?"

She sipped on a can of Canada Dry.

"There's no signal out here," he said. "It's been like two hours since we last saw a phone tree."

"Why'd you start a conversation with that weirdo?" she asked. At Gazoo's, they'd encountered an old woman with fine silver jewelry on her fingers.

"She made me laugh," he said.

"You paid her a dollar for a wish," she said.

"That's what she was selling," he said. "That's what I bought."

The sunbeams and shadows played off her sunglasses. They drove in silence.

"So, what…" she asked, eventually. "What did you wish for?"

He blushed. Embarrassed. "Wouldn't you like to know?" he said.

She thought about it for a moment. "Fuck you," she said.

The entrance to the park was just a log cabin and a sign. A ranger stacked kindling onto an ATV. The man got out and waved. "How ya doin'?" Justin said.

The ranger stopped and took off his work gloves. "Can't complain."

Justin tried his cell phone again, but there was still no reception. He put his phone away. "We have a reservation," he said.

The ranger looked around. "Take any spot you like," he said. "They're all plenty good." He scanned their full car. "Would you like some wood? Forecast calls for rain."

Sarah got out. "Do you take credit cards?" she asked.

"Sorry, cash only," the ranger said.

"Oh crap," said Justin.

The ranger had figured as much. "Don't sweat it," he said. "Take some of the offcuts. It'll keep you warm."

Sarah moved a hair lock from her eyes. "Thank you," she said. All that was great and good in people. It had been a while.

They drove up a peninsula. A backbone road. At the mouth, a white fishing boat was anchored. They heard loud clangs as machines unloaded the catch. The campsite smelled of cut grass. No one was there, except for a father and his two bickering kids. They were annoying. As they set up their tent, Sarah and Justin followed their example, and argued loudly.

Later, as they put out the rest of their sleeping gear, they didn't speak.

She read an old paperback that she'd grabbed from a motel. He couldn't stand being stuck in an enclosed nylon space. So he threw on a wetsuit, and left. She hated him, but she hated being alone more. So she fumbled with her neoprene and got her hair caught in the zipper.

"Wait," she shouted. But he'd already disappeared down the trail.

She pushed through the red spruce trees. Pine needles scratched her face. He stood at the water's edge. Dipping his toes in the water. "Water's cold," he said. A speedboat with a happy family shot past. Waving. Racing the setting sun.

She saw the trawler better now. It looked like a monument. Clanging. It had blue trim. The water was frigid. "Damn," she said. Beneath the surface, a huge crab scuttled past her toes. She wasn't surprised. She was numb. Justin put on his goggles and tried to find the crustacean's hiding place.

The sun set as they climbed back to the campsite. They pulled off their wetsuits like selkies. Like second skins. They hadn't bathed in days. But the cold made her hair smell new. She cried. She wasn't sure why. "Oh come on," Justin said. Again, he struggled with the tent fly. "Work, dammit." He got it to work, then stepped out of the tent.

She changed by herself. She heard the family arguing at the other end of the campsite. She wished they knew how lucky they were.

There were no stars. It was cool and humid. Justin used the offcuts to light a fire.

They waited for the water to boil. He cut slices of baloney. "I wish we had some marshmallows," he said.

"And graham crackers and chocolate," she said. "Everyone loves s'mores."

"Why is there an H in Graham?" he asked. "When everyone says *gram.*" This was him at his most pedantic.

"I think it's someone's name," she said.

He added the noodles to the boiling water. "Yeah, but the name has a *ha* to it," he said.

She threw a twig into the fire. "It's kids," she said. "They pronounce it with a mouth full of marshmallow." She mimicked a mouth full of goo. "Grammmm."

He put the lid on the pot. "I think we should pronounce the H. In honor of Mr. Graham and his delicious crackers."

She felt tired. "Write someone a letter," she said. They ate their noodles in silence. She picked a hair out of her bowl. It rained. He doused the flames. She hid the dirty dishes in the trunk. They didn't want another visit from a bear. They'd deal with the dishes in the morning.

He still struggled with the zipper. "Cheap Walmart shit," he complained. "Nothing's dry."

"Oh, great outdoorsman," Sarah said. She turned on the lantern. "Everything looks overgrown," she said. She toweled off her head and tossed him the beach towel.

"It's sandy," he said.

She bit her lip. "Tell me something nice," she said.

"Not annoying?" he said.

She unbuttoned her fleece. It smelled like bug spray. "Tell me something nice about *me.*"

He pushed his glasses up his nose, and dried the rainwater off his stubble. "I like the sound you make when you can't get a Wordle…It's a squeak snort."

She threw a sleeping bag at him. "A snort!' she said. "That's all you got?"

He squinted like he was trying to crush her with his eyelids. "I don't know what you want from me," he said.

She lay down on her sleeping mat. "I don't know. I just…" She pulled lint out of her belly button. "Can you just not *be* yourself," she said.

He listened to the rain fall on the nylon. "I love that you still bite your lips when you think about…"

She kissed him. It was the first time that they had kissed since. It surprised him. He had to catch his breath. He kissed her back. He slipped his hand under her fleece. And felt her shoulder blades. Her skin was still cold from the swim.

They took off their shirts. "Can you hold me a bit," she said.

Their limbs tangled. And they lay there locked in silence. Listening to the rain. To the occasional *clang.* He thought about the sound that crab made when it scurried over the rocks. A sort of *clack clack* under the water. His fingers squeezed harder…but she felt different. He plucked a single hair off her shoulder. "Ow," she said.

He stared at the single hair on the tip of his finger.

"Why did you do that?" she said.

"They say your hair keeps growing after…" he said.

"I don't want to think about that," she said. She put her shirt back on.

"Sarah, your shoulders are hairy," he said.

She grabbed Justin's hand. "That's a weird thing to say," she said.

"Touch your back," he said.

She didn't like to touch herself. But she also didn't like how he was staring at her.

She grabbed at her shoulder, and tugged at her skin. He was right. She had back hair. That was weird. Growing old?

"They say hair is good luck…" he said.

She threw her raincoat at him. Then, she bent forward and moved her left hand to the crook of her back.

It was covered in fur. Luscious hair like a '70s folk singer. She pulled her hand away.

"Jesus," she said. She touched her back again. It was hirsute. "Justin," she said, "your face."

He pressed his fingers to his face. His stubble had grown into a full beard. Like a mountain man. He fumbled through their rucksacks, and pulled out the bag of toiletries. "I'm like Mr. Natural looking for the right tool," he said. He flipped open her compact mirror. "Holy shit," he said. He looked like a grizzled prospector.

"Throw me the multitool," she said. The blade wasn't sharp enough. And the scissors got tangled after a few snips. He opened his bag and pulled out his good knife. The one his brother got him as a wedding present.

"Lie down," she said. Using the Gerber knife, she cut his beard. A clean shave.

But, still, the hair came down in great torrents. Like a river run. With salmon in it.

The hair engulfed their bodies and stretched out on their clothes.

"It's getting tight," she moaned.

"Get my pants off," he begged.

They tore off their clothes.

"It's stuck," he grunted. "I can't get it…"

She took his utility knife and cut off her hikers. She looked like a yeti.

He dug out their medical kit, the yellow one, waterproof, with the red cross, and extracted the surgical scissors. He thrashed at her hair with them. The hair gushed out like they'd struck oil. Eventually the joint wore out, and he had to use the scissor arm like a blade. He hacked and sawed at her rivulets of hair till the blade dulled.

She lost the knife. It was buried deep in his beard.

He found the BBQ lighter, a Hail Mary, and tried to burn his hair away. It just stank. And it hurt.

And so she gently, tenderly placed her hand on the Zippo, and said, "Please, let's just go to bed." He flicked it closed and tossed it aside.

Exhausted, they lay down together on their inflatable mattresses.

"You always said that I was too hairy," he said.

She listened to his heartbeat. "I was wrong," she said. "You look good in a beard."

He howled at the moon. She laughed.

"That's a lie," he said. "I look like a slob."

And then their hair turned white. He held a lock of hers in his fingers. "It's the color of your mother's," he said. "She always said that I would turn gray before my forties."

She looked into his face. She thought about how weird the word hirsute was.

"I thought you were only going to say nice things to me?" she said.

He touched her chin. "I did. I loved your mother's hair."

And she held him like someone else. Someone hirsute. Someone covered in hair.

And it came out of their belly buttons. Like tree roots. And it came out of their armpits. As bushes and vines. It came out of his penis. Like brambles. And when the pubic hair rushed out of her vagina. She groaned. And there were wildflowers. And she held it. And it cried. She held it to her chest and she nursed it. And they were a family again.

The hair kept them warm. And the storm washed the hair. It smelled of sea salt. In the morning, the world was fresh and new.

BABE

gray lindsey

First I have you,
like a good idea or nightmare,
clinging, clinging till I find a way
to falsify—like I could have
something of my own without—

You turn one today.
Younger than breathing, the act
or the stopping of, but older than
the marigolds in our kitchen window.

Theories like you are impossible
to squash.

I try every day, when the light hits
just right and your little arms reach out
for a name—no name
that comforts me—and I choke you
till you are older, finally,
than breathing.
Then I have another one
just like you, or maybe
nothing like you—
I don't ever absorb the details.
I do it again, infanticide at twilight
and labor at dawn. This is a parent's job,

to hold the murder weapon
so no one else does.

Fiction

A WOMAN IS SCREAMING

Joe Koch

SOMEONE MUST have broken in. She'd never have left the door unlatched, much less ajar, with a naked sliver of her private life available from a certain angle to anyone sly enough to notice as they walked by. It wasn't like her to miss a step in her routine, important or minor, and certainly not a step so vital as securing her front door before venturing forth. Maybe she'd forgotten the deadbolt now and then, or, lulled into a sense of safety over time, she'd allowed habitual familiarity with this known location where she'd so long eluded violence or harassment to embolden her. She'd be deliberately careless sometimes, she who should know better, by her profession and hard-earned wisdom, know better than to tempt fate.

She'd revel in defying her conditioned fear, declare herself recovered and impervious and go to the laundry room to start a load without locking up, or run down to the lobby to retrieve a package. Across the street to grab a snack.

The thrill of such small freedoms, saying fuck off into the sun to hypervigilance, the luxury of risk; but not this morning, not today. Not all day long at work and into the evening after dinner and drinks with friends and stretching out to ten or twelve hours of absence baring her home to strangers, her property to assault. She wouldn't go that far.

She wouldn't try to resurrect the past and give it a makeover or recast the roles so that someone else suffers the damage this time around. She's not cruel like that. Emotion doesn't drive her, or if it does, it's a many-layered costume restricting the sensationalism of arousal, nausea, and tears required by listeners whose sympathy frankly angers her more than it helps, and so she has disposed of the costume and often gone silent, wearing instead no emotion that anyone else can understand.

She's stepped back from the door with a gasp. Leapt back, really. One sharp gasp and then she holds her breath. Her key still points at the doorknob, the ring and carabiners gripped tightly in her hand, the cool metal of the keys warming as her palm floods with its own animal instincts and sends an alarm signal translated as sweat.

If she goes inside, she knows how the story goes. A killer or rapist awaits.

Stillness behind the door, its dark green surface suddenly wildly alive to her scanning eyes. Layers repainted hastily between tenants have accumulated over time into a thick, writhing texture coating the old wood in a false liquid sheen. Droplets escape containment to spot the hardware. Crevices and drips unsanded for ages and lumping like green pustules, more and more of them the longer she stares in hypervigilance, an infected skin over her threshold she has touched daily, without giving it a thought. Daily, she hasn't noticed how it undulates. A skin ready to burst.

This threatening plane that encases her safety now splits. Two and a half inches of darkness from top to bottom, a grey slice of twilight where a murderer or sex criminal hides.

Or maybe a maintenance man for relief not quite comic, but calling into question every suspicion she has yet to express. Every wolf she has cried under her breath. Someone will laugh at her, at her perceived overreaction to the warnings of subtle stimuli only she can detect. They'll mock her cowardice and write off crimes yet to happen, unaware that her stomach now digests them in advance like a meal of concrete.

Someone will emerge to laugh at her distress. Someone who has never been bitten bites hardest, though she's often been surprised by how brutally the camaraderie of survivors demands evidence.

If she hesitates or asks for help, she's weak and foolish. If she goes inside, she's to blame for being careless. Asking for it. Or maybe she's more perverse, braving the set piece with its gratuitous violence to expose the truth kept just off camera, just out of plain sight.

Maybe every home contains a rapist. Maybe we're all killers in the dark.

Every woman she's seen murdered on screen deserves an audience, but this is not how it happens in real life. Even if it's only the maintenance man, even if he's come and gone and left a receipt of radiators drained or skylight caulked, she'll hesitate the next day before putting on her underwear, wondering if he's fondled them. Her shoulders will tense when she gets in bed, uncertain if she can smell a stranger's scent, and if the indentation visible in the blankets was there when she left in a rush for work that morning, or if he has rubbed his body on this spot where she now curls, rigid, unable to sleep. She'll have scrubbed the bathroom repeatedly, staying up much too late, trying to make sure every smear of toothpaste or soap on the basin is removed and sterilized with bleach in case the stain isn't soap or toothpaste, in case this is where he chose to masturbate.

She'll give up trying to sleep and throw everything in a laundry basket and then stand paralyzed inside the apartment, holding it against her hip with one fist around the basket's grip and her other hand on the doorknob, unmoving. Willing her wrist to turn or her fingers to go through the necessary motions, yet remaining at this impasse in the imagined anxiety of the near future, mirroring her anxiety and frozen inaction right now as she peers into the long, dark shadow of the unknown, the thin gap between jamb and door.

Her life inside unmoving, invisible, invaded, the broken barrier revealing inchoate grey behind the writhing green paint; it may be the stillness of absence, the stillness of expectation, or the stillness of an impatient fate. What grows in that grey as she hovers, clutching her handbag and junk-mail against her chest, her chest hardly moving, once again breathing, yet breathing so quietly, so softly and shallowly; what grows in the grey imperceptibly shifts.

Within the shadows, something assembles into form as she discovers her breath.

The whisper of stockings on legs that cross and uncross, a flicker of mistaken identity that mimics the light and dark of the grey as it is chopped up by passing traffic through parted curtains and window sheers. She leans closer. The lights go quiet.

Another woman.

If the shadows can leak out through this sliver, the other woman could approach the door and throw it open. Swiftly, her legs will scissor across carpet. Her slender hand is urgent and deft. She rips the green skin from the threshold.

Confronting the intruder, will the woman within see her own face? Will she who stands outside erupt from her interminable pause into apologies, pleas, or threats? Most importantly to the frozen lurker on the threshold, which of these two women will wield the knife?

In any scene like this, she knows the rule: there must be a blonde and a brunette. They don't represent good and evil, or Madonna and whore, or any other common dichotomy assigned by tradition or popular culture. There's no vulgar or implicit meaning to the color of the wigs or to which one wears which. The necessity of a simple shorthand for differentiation demands their use, especially if the face is the same as she fears it will be if the light changes and chops again, or if she continues to lean ever closer to the slit of shadow, and with a gentle, surreptitious push she increases the angle of access enough to catch herself unawares, the other woman who sniffles in resignation and pretends to herself she's not still shaking as she changes out of her torn things and stuffs them in the trash. Or maybe the wig slips and she looks up, aware she is being watched, aware her life now has no barriers. Her home has been displaced.

Outside, her stomach rumbles with disgust from chewing on its own fear, another animal part with its own agenda like her slick, cold hand clenching the keyring, another warning sign that her suspended animation can't outlast the violence or destiny or joke that is being played upon her. The hallway can't remain neutral forever, has never been truly neutral in fact as she can see by the inconsistency of the dim nipple of overhead light and the scuffs and gouges repaired or not in the plaster. Everywhere, the brutality of constant action has left scars that refuse to let her cocoon and heal.

The flooring is hard in high heels, loud like an alarm when from her sweating, unstable fingers the keys clatter out of her grip. Loud like an alarm when her feet should say run, run before the door opens and she catches you, or you her, or he drags you inside and changes your future, or ends it. Run, before you see the face behind the killer's green mask.

Her feet like stubborn children whine in their high heels as her arches and toes cramp. Below her, the keys sink. The doorway is submerged below water now, and this odd development seems unshocking to her, a problem easy enough to fix.

She releases her feet from their leather straps and stacks the shoes beside her junk-mail and handbag on the doormat. The sigh of her skirts as she bends down to dive doesn't tell her reliably if she is the brunette or the blonde, and at this moment she can't remember. She's been both at one time or another, both the woman and the other, and the water is too clouded with the building's crumbling decay and the evidence of age to give her a hint by reflection of which she will be tonight. If she looks at a long strand to decide, she won't be able to distinguish wigs from truth from dye jobs, because there are many forms of deception that occur when a killer is on the loose.

Ingenious in her disguise, she dives fully clothed despite her outfit's tasteful elegance and the potential damage to its carefully chosen fabrics, despite the extra weight of sodden layers that will hinder her freedom of movement and control of her limbs as she swims. She holds her breath and sinks down, realizing she doesn't need her keys anymore and never will again, for the grey has swallowed her through its slender mouth and taken her in past the bubbling green skin.

That frivolous door-skin has hardly been a barrier to harm, offering protection as it has in the paradoxical configuration of a way in. It now dissipates completely under the water like the illusion it has always been.

In liquid shadow she hangs suspended, floating below her ceiling and holding her breath. Her less weighty household things drift in the murk as the deep green droplets tint and obscure her surroundings, encasing the apartment in the fog of an underwater forest. She waves both arms to shift position, pushing against what suspends her and aching toward progress. Black needles poke at her lungs with a fervent desire for air, but she has incredible self-control and will resist this instinct like so many other instincts that have failed to serve her in the past.

The past is what has sunk her in this nightmare cliché, and like the cliché she seems fated to embrace, she makes for the kitchen and, with a hand no longer slick with sweat but firm in the murk, pulls a knife from the block and holds it up.

A fast figure or shadow flows past from behind. She catches the change in light and turns. Curtains or waves suggest the intruder's path.

Pushing away at stubborn water with her arms, with the crisscross kicking of her sheer-stockinged feet, she fights the delay of her heavy garments and the piercing need in her lungs. Pursuing the intruder into the bedroom, knife raised, hair afloat, eyes burning in the dirty water; no one. Closet empty, corners uninhabited. Nothing under the bed. Until a hand reaches from under the blankets above, brushing the back of her neck.

She jolts up, though the jolt is slow, impeded by her state of immersion. Beneath undulating bedclothes, her body, her other body, her hand of waterlogged and plastic-looking, of distant and puzzling flesh set adrift and jutting from her bloated body. The other woman body-melting in fast-forward decay. The woman locked behind the door in fear.

Bubbles empty the body of gasses and the skin deflates, caving in over deliquescing organ and protruding bone. She drops the knife. It floats. The wig slips, but it is the body's scalp sloughing away, not a fake, neither blonde or brunette, sliding into invisible murk like an octopus, unveiling her bone pate. Pulling away the used rag of her face.

She cries out into the muffling water, a drowned cry that no one but she can hear. The corpse's fear doesn't faze her. She claims it. She throws her arms around the other, lifts it from the bed intent on rescue, lugging the torso out, out, out.

Deteriorated tissues unravel with each kick through the liquid gloom. Bones detach and drift or settle. The skeleton comes apart, leaving only the empty skull clasped lovingly and grievingly against her chest.

If those lips could speak, they might ask her if, once opened, a door can't be closed; or is it the other way around? They might break free through the green skin of liquid and make a sound. But because this submerged ending is reality and the nightmare holds her frozen before an unlocked door, neither open nor closed but ajar, she returns alone to the impasse at the threshold where she stands in singular paralysis, key raised and pointed toward the shadow-sliver, the gap.

She can't make a sound when the hall, never neutral and now aggressively insistent, echoes as the realtor approaches with a potential tenant. She can't resist their passage when the two of them walk through her and into the ectoplasm where she floats.

They don't see the disarray she's left behind, the months of trash not taken out, of laundry re-worn and then rinsed, of clothes and underwear left draped over every surface to dry stiff. They don't recognize it is she wielding knives at thin air in the dark, or shivering as she grows emaciated on the bed where her blankets offer too little protection and she pushes the dresser and nightstands and couch and coffee table against the front door, and then the fridge when it's empty, every lamp, every book, every chair.

They don't hear her cry out when she finds herself, though if the new tenant has pets like the one before and the others before that, a dog or a cat might stare intently at the front door on certain evenings. They might refuse to eat in one particular corner of the kitchen where the stains have been erased, and whine or mewl long into the night and go suddenly silent at the foot of the bed.

ASK A NECROMANCER: C'EST ICI DE L'EMPIRE DE LA MORT

Amanda Downum

Like any necromancer, I've dreamed of building an empire of the dead. Or maybe at least a nice bone tower—I don't support colonialism, and I've never felt cut out for government administration. So it came as a surprise even to me when I started plotting a cadaver revolution that involves…grant writing.

I've written before about tissue donation, mostly in a facile way describing the challenges it creates for embalmers. (There is nothing facile about embalming a bone donor, I promise.) What I didn't go into was whole body donation. Whole body donation—or anatomical donation, as it will be recorded on your death certificate—means donating your body to science. Mary Roach discusses this in her book *Stiff*, which I still haven't read yet, despite owning a copy.

When I started my Gross Anatomy class in mortuary school, we took a field trip to the University of Texas at San Antonio to pick up our cadavers from their anatomical donation program. I had no idea how anatomical embalming worked, and no exposure yet to traditional embalming with which to compare. We spent that semester dissecting those cadavers and memorizing a truly unholy number of muscles, ligaments, and vessels. One of our cadavers had an unusual pathological heart condition, and many nursing students filed through like ducklings to marvel at it. In Texas, mortuary schools are allowed to embalm for funeral homes, so that Gross Anatomy lab was my only exposure to anatomical donation while in school.

In Virginia, funeral service programs can obtain cadavers only from the State Anatomical Program. VSAP provides cadavers to all the medical and allied health programs that offer wet labs. Although VSAP is a state agency, they're entirely self-funded, which means they recoup operational expenses through the sale of cadavers. I begrudge them not one obol, and their laboratory manager certainly deserves a raise. The problem, though, is that cadavers are expensive, and I work at a poor community college. The more our cadavers cost, the more fuss we get about our yearly budget.

I keep threatening to give our business office a lecture about Burke and Hare, but my dean hasn't signed off on it yet.

Not every medical system or health program has the facilities to maintain a wet lab, so occasionally bartering occurs. We share some cadavers with another program, they trade us a bag of flour and a goat, etc. Sharing our lab facilities with community partners always makes the college feel nice. My office is next door to the EMS Program Director's, and I've made an alliance between first and last responders. Their students get to practice lifesaving procedures on something besides a dummy or a chicken leg, and my students get to learn about all the things they'll encounter when EMS fails to save a particular life.

My networking attempts started as a way to potentially increase the number of cadavers I can order in a semester, so I don't have to share one body amongst fifteen students like a beleaguered carrion bird feeding too many fledglings. It turns out, though, that I feel quite passionately about cadaver labs and access thereto. Some people dream of donating their body to science and helping find a cure for cancer, or some other specific disease—and that is a valid dream. But donating your body and helping a class full of surgical students better understand anatomy is equally valid. Or helping a class of EMS students learn to place an IO port without flinching, or intubate a patient smoothly, or perform a cricothyroidotomy or thoracostomy in the field to keep someone alive until they get to the hospital. I will always argue for the importance of deathcare in any field, whether nursing or mortuary science, but even those morticians who denigrate funeral embalming might have a hard time explaining why medical students shouldn't learn on a real human body.

As part of my Master's of Public Health program, I took a Project Management for Public Health class. If that sounds joyless to you, it did to me as well. Luckily, the class focused on grant writing, and the professor was delightful. My mock grant proposal for the semester was pursuing a cadaver grant (at least one exists!) to start an anatomical research alliance. I have no idea how realistic this enterprise is, but I'm just a necromancer with a big dream. A job for every corpse; a cadaver for every school!

Fiction

SOLE

Aliya Whiteley

WILL THIS letter reach you? I don't know yet.

That's the familiar response. It's the answer that passes responsibility for my words to time. Time, the inarguable overlord of our relationship, all relationships. But you know me well, you always have. I like the familiar. You sigh at how I guard our sacred Sunday mornings and hold their pattern inviolable. I won't change our schedule. Waking up late and walking for an hour through the city sees both of us at our best.

For you and me, the Sunday morning city is a forest.

Me, in a reverie provided by the well-worn path, as if springy earth had been tamped down over the years of our predictable travels, leaf mulch under our feet. Buildings long established, dates on the façades, tall and straight as trunks. And you, pointing out the smaller details, looking left and right for wondrous ephemeral things, the tight yellows and pinks, blue stripes and red caps of the joggers like the flashes of bright birds across the journey. The Sunday expedition to our regular coffee shop for brunch. Some places find their power in being the destination: the aftermath of the arrival. The quiet ground. We always talk well to each other over brunch.

Your hair is a mess from the crosstown wind, it has worked free from its clip, curling where it hits your shoulders, and you are alive, alert, and ready to order something special. A celebration. Of what? Of seeing a lesser-spotted rollerblader, speedy, nimble, dressed in a polka-dot one-piece and cheeping along to the music in their head. But I want to stick to the usual, so we do.

You say you'd like to live in a forest. But you laugh at yourself, you know it's ridiculous. You like your contemporary comforts and your job, too. You don't want to spend the time commuting. You say you're too lazy to have things any other way, and I agree, but it worries me. Am I the easy course of action, too? The comfortable, if not spectacular

I'm off track. I'll start this letter again.

I want to sit at this table, in our usual coffee shop, and describe to you what the city looked like this Sunday morning, after I left the apartment. That hour of walking. Because we always thought the city and the forest were irreconcilable, which was why we played the game of imagining one as the other. Two completely different ways of living. What I mean by that is

I'll start again again.

We take a midweek trip to the New Forest, on the South Coast. It's two hours away. We sit on either side of the table in a busy carriage on a slow stopper train, and watch the way the view unscrolls, as if cranked mechanically in front of the window. We move from the gleam of the new developments of the city to the small rows of houses, their gardens holding forgotten play equipment and the skeletal remains of last year's Christmas trees. Then sudden breaks of open fields, expanse of sky with scudding clouds that threaten yet more rain, and swollen rivers, and foliage half-swallowed in ponds, and yes it rains every day we spend in the New Forest and we walk so far in it, joking that what it really needs is a coffee shop. But jokes are rare, there. You're not a fan of jokes, really. You like the sound of rain on cupped leaves, running down the ragged lines of the trunks, wet and rough. I think the sound of rainfall is not so different from the lull of night traffic through our bedroom window, always left ajar. Both can lull me to sleep.

Today the coffee shop is playing light jazz, peppered with tinkling piano. I've ordered our usual: a sharing plate of pancakes with cream and mixed berries. The berries are sour in the spring. There's a daffodil in a vase on every one of the round silver tables, and scattered newspaper supplements to pick up at leisure. On the table next to me there's a fashion pull-out, models preening. The date shows it's from the week before. I'm so tired. Waiting for the caffeine to kick in.

The city. We were so wrong about the city. We thought it was unconquerable, concrete, written in stone, cement and estrangement. We thought we belonged to it: to urban glass and metal expectations.

You say to me—a rare comment to break the sound of the endless rain on the leaves—that you could stay here forever, a creature of the New Forest. I point out that you wouldn't last a day. Which berries are safe to eat? I point to a bush of dark long leaves and bright red punctuations. You tell me you'll stick to the berries on Sunday morning sharing pancakes. For some reason this comment makes me remember that your parents are richer than mine. I come from the poor side of the city, and for a moment I think that might translate to survival, as if I can outlast you in any situation.

Well. We both now know that's true.

I'll start again.

I want to write about my walk through the city, from front door to coffee shop. One hour of walking. The berries are sour, the pancakes sweet, the coffee rich, a little bitter, as always, and the hit of the caffeine is coming, it's beginning to seep through the crack of the window. Listen, here's the thing, you fucking idiot, you have always lived in the forest, you're alive in it now. I can see you.

You're also lying in the ground in a tasteful facility where they planted a tree on top of you, and your mother asked what kind of tree you would have wanted and I had to admit defeat, to say—after my insistence upon the tree burial idea, she loved trees, she was always happiest among trees—that you have never once named a specific tree as your favourite and you know nothing about trees, not really, except that you once went on a holiday to the New Forest and liked the sound of the rain on the cupped leaves, and liked the feel of bark under your fingers. Your mother chose apple. The man at the tasteful facility said apple saplings tend to do well, although roughly a third of all the saplings don't take, but when that happens, they'll provide a replacement sapling for free.

Your mother asks me if I'm certain this is what you wanted, and I tell her I don't know yet. But perhaps that's not quite true. You loved the forest, you wanted to live in the forest. It's only that I couldn't bear to take what remains of you to the New Forest and surreptitiously slip you under the trees, then take a two-hour stopper train back without you. I want you close. I continue to want you close.

Yes, this is a letter to tell you: I'm so fucking angry.

The city, you love it, you won't admit it, our life is here, in the city. You belong to it because you belong with me. You say everything is fresh and whole and perfect in the forest, breathe it in, breathe deep, and you breathed deep, but you were already compromised, the disease had slipped in through the crack in the window and put its roots inside you. You never belonged in a forest. I have no idea why I insisted on putting a tree upon you. It'll probably feed on your remains, take on your sickness, and die. We'll be replanting in less than a year. If you ever loved me, you loved the city. The city as it was, for us, before it changed.

I'll start again.

This morning, as soon as I set foot outside the front door, I knew the city was different. Not to look at, not at first. But it was inside me, this realisation that I was not looking at the same street, the same shop windows and parked cars with permits, and the same full bins and ripped billboards, even though they are the same to see, with the surface level unaltered.

I locked the door and started walking, and it occurred to me that I felt this alteration not in my core, or any comfortable idiocy of that kind, I don't believe in that, you know I never have, but the change was radiating up through my feet. My soles rather than my soul, if you like, although you would have rolled your eyes at that joke. My letter, my rules. No, the city had changed below its visible layer, deep in its foundations.

I crossed at our usual spot, where the cars slow to turn into the multi-story, and I dodged between the joggers and roller-bladers along the riverside way. With every step the feeling increased, and by the time I reached the third blue bench I couldn't ignore it any longer. I sat and let the rhythm of the change beneath me surge: soles, ankles, knees, hips, heart. I put my hand on my chest and breathed in time. It wasn't enough. I had to get closer. I moved from the bench to the ground and lay flat, face down, my forehead on the asphalt between the bench and the nearest bin. I could smell the many discarded things in the bin, mingling, making a familiar scent of dog poo bags, beer cans, fast food wrappers, encasements, disposables, all above ground and intact, reeking of city life, but below, below, the city was newly aware of me, and growing.

A voice asked me if I was okay.

Imagine that, in this city.

I sat up and said I was. The jogger was a common grey warbler with blue cap. He nodded and moved away, resuming his comfortable pace, and I knew then that what was happening below was affecting above, in a good way. Cities have roots, and roots grow and change and convey their messages, and push their energy into the structures above.

I noticed a small plant growing through a crack between the kerb and the road, using the shelter of the bin. It was nothing more than a springy stick with one long leaf. A possibility. A sapling? I don't know yet. Maybe it'll turn into a tree. And I stood up and looked around and saw shoots of green everywhere, dotted like a pattern, a puzzle to be solved. Weeds in the cracks, lifting the heaviest stones.

That is the change in the city. That is the change in me.

You're part of this change. I sense your cupped hand in it. I feel you listening. I'm aware of you, under the soles of my feet. I was right to plant you, close, like a possibility.

The coffee is wearing off. I'm tired again. It's a long walk back across the city, alone, but there will be green spring growth for company.

I want to write you a letter about how you belong to the city and the forest. You are both, because one day they might be the same thing. Does that make sense? I don't know yet.

YOU BUILD YOUR HOUSE ON YOUR FATHER'S CORPSE

Sadoeuphemist

YOU BUILD your house on your father's corpse. The grounds are overgrown with patches of bramble and thorn—your father was a hairy man. The foundations, its borders, are shifting, amorphous. The tides come in and wash away the shore. Your house is built on a bedrock of flaking shale. Yes indeed, this is your father's body: his chest, his arms, the degrading slope of his gut. You walk down the hill to draw water, and you have to watch your footing. Navigating your father's corpse is a perilous affair.

The grounds are worse at night. There are no creatures that chirp or scurry in the darkness, nothing to accompany you but silence. Your father's corpse in the dark is indistinguishable from shadow. You can see him in the hollows of the caves, in the spaces between brambles, atop rocks slouched together as a throne, as if the very emptiness itself takes on a mass and weight and form. By daylight you unearth rocks streaked through with veins of iron already corroding in the moist earth, stinking of rust and sulfur. You strike iron against flint. You make fire. You carry a flickering torch with you when venturing out after dark, and the landscape shifts according to where you shine your light, hillocks and boulders and outcroppings of rock all invisible until they are banging against your knees and shins, threatening to topple you over. Shadows dematerialize and re-form, stones emerge and are swallowed up again into the ground. You are navigating a restless sea, one that shrinks at your gaze and wells up everywhere else.

You had once lived in a cave, a grotto, a hollow sunken into your father's gut. It was raining when you first came here; there was a squall. You lifted your head and yowled into the storm, thrilled and terrified and utterly free. The rain was hot and stung your face, and you welcomed it. The cave was less refuge than a promise of shelter to come. Sweat beaded on the walls and cooled in rivulets down the pockmarked stone, leaving the inside of the cave both feverish and clammy. You curled up against a patch of matted lichen and listened to the rain, slowly succumbing to exhaustion. The walls and floor curved around you, cradled you, and in that way you slept.

Your father's corpse is mostly rich and fertile, at points sinking into bog. Grass grows everywhere—yes, there is bramble; yes, even the blades of grass are stiff and sharp and curving and scratch at your legs and thighs—but there are also wild stalks of wheat and millet and corn, clusters of grapes dangling from the vine, black tomatoes taut with juice, the skin bulging beneath your thumb. Once you uproot the weeds and brambles, the earth settles itself into striated furrows, ready for planting. You have made primitive tools, rocks painstakingly chipped away into sharpened edges, their black surface rippled with whorls. You lash them to sticks. You make an ax, a spear, an adz—or at least the crude approximations of them. You drive your blade into the earth and it almost bleeds.

The trees are black, the grass is black, the corn is black; all that grows here is varying shades of black, all except for the dead. One out of every three stalks comes up pale and lifeless, stunted at germination. You go through the rows and weed out the white stalks, and they come out at the root. They crumple in your hands, hollow and rustling. You hack down a white tree, and inside there is dust and dry rot. So much of what you grow is useless. Ghostly shapes watch you from the woods, bulbous and loping and pinheaded, their faces like the barest glimpse of sun from the bottom of a well. They bound away, skittish like deer. When you investigate, you find cool clear springwater welling up from where they once stood.

The first time you kill one, it is almost by accident. An afternoon spent crouched in the tall grass, waiting, watching their movements, scarcely daring to breathe. They mill about almost mindlessly, like water droplets creeping down a pane of glass. Tentative, gathering momentum, tracing each other's tracks. When you finally lunge forward, spear in hand, it is less attack than a surprise. Your thrust goes wild and hits air. They scatter. A slender leg catches on an arched root, a joint splinters backwards. One of the creatures crumples to the ground. The membrane of its flank stretches taut as it sucks air, expands, deflates, a dying pulse fluttering through its body.

It takes minutes to die. You feel sick looking at it. Its skin peels off in cloudy, translucent strips, coming apart in your hands. It does not bleed. An oily serum seeps up from its flayed musculature, clear and weeping. Its flesh crisps over the fire, turning a carbonized brown. Shards of it stick between your teeth.

It is the extremities of your father's corpse that offer the most opportunity for exploration, rocky, callused promontories stretching out into the sea. The stones are blunt and hostile and dig into the soles of your feet. There is grit collecting beneath your father's nails, barnacles and chitons and small meaty mussels, tiny gray shrimp with black polluted veins running along their spines. All the creatures of the land, the things that pass as rabbit and deer and quail, have clear delicate bones, white bloodless flesh that reminds you more of fish. It is the creatures of the sea that are truly redolent of meat, the metallic tang of iron heavy on your tongue. They stain the lines in your hands black as you slit them open and extract their entrails, spreading them out to dry in the sun. Exposed sheets of coral stand brittle and yellowing above the waves, sun-bleached and flaking. Ships have torn themselves to pieces against your father's corpse, leaving flotsam wedged among the rocks, and although you have kept your eyes peeled towards the horizon you have never seen an intact ship sailing, never found another survivor. You are surrounded by ghosts.

You have a bounty to salvage.

Sand eats everything. Sand swarms over the wreckage, teeming from crack and crevasse as you dislodge your finds. The grains, held up to the sun, are translucent husks, rough with ragged limb and pedipalp. Whatever microscopic creatures lived here once have since molted, embryonic flesh emerging from the shell, leaving home for better prospects. The shore is a graveyard of their former lives. Sand grits between your toes, clings to the folds in your skin.

You dislodge gray and waterlogged planks, splintered and uneven, more than enough to build your house. You lug them up the shore, picking splinters from your palms, and then scavenge frayed lengths of rope to lash them together in bundles, fixing together a crude sledge to haul behind you. A curved section of hull becomes a roof, half a hovel to crouch under and sort through your haul. There are treasures, of course, ivory dentures and cufflinks and spectacle frames with the lenses dashed out, all sorts of trinkets that are largely useless to you. The sea brings you furnishings: a legless chest of drawers to be propped up against a tree trunk, three-legged chairs, scarred tabletops and battered copper pots, miraculously intact bottles, a tattered knot of fabrics that must have once been a chest of clothes.

The wood is rotten, the metal rough with corrosion, the cloth stringy with holes. The accumulation of lifetimes, reduced to so much detritus. You drag them up the hillside and begin to assemble the tentative outlines of a house, like tracing out a constellation through long-dead stars. This is what has washed to the surface. There is more still lying in the depths.

You swim through hidden coves, run your hand across glistening cavern walls. There are broken white stones you have clung to and dived off from, arranged in jagged semicircles; there are vortices and bloodstains and gaps. There are points of suction, undertow. You nearly drowned once, sucked down into a darkness that blotted out all light, and your foot pushed off against what felt like a rubbery carpet of kelp, or perhaps the back of an impossibly large tentacle. Perhaps it moved, or perhaps it was merely your fear that made it so. You came up gasping and vomiting water. There are networks of sunken caves beneath the water, impossibly deep and complex. Who knows what things have drowned down there, what dissolving corpses filter up to the surface. The waves break against the stones in a constant spray of mist that stings at your shoulders and face. Whenever you are down here, you feel as if you will never again be dry. You have delved between the crevasses of the rocks for treasure and come away with silver, come away with handfuls of flaking coral. The lip of the cove is lined with spiny urchins and sea stars and anemones. You stab yourself with their venom each time you leave.

You salvage a silver pocket watch, corroded gears gritted together in their glossy shell, a set of silverware gleaming like slats of moonlight. As well, a kit of rusted tools: a hammer, auger, saw blade, dozens upon dozens of iron nails. Now that the weather has cooled, new figures skulk through your father's corpse. They are long-legged and pale, much like the deer in the forest; unlike the deer, long-fingered and upright. They are inquisitive, and bolder than any of the others. Their footsteps do not crush grass. They approach the edges of your clearing in the dark of night.

The first time they came, you were asleep.

You had spent a long day scavenging, hauling, sorting, fitting together, laying stones to mark the boundary of your field. Your house was a hollow tree back then: an upstairs in the branches, planks laid out across them to make floorboards. You had pulled yourself upstairs at the end of the day and fell back on a mattress of dried stalks, sinking into sleep beneath the pinpricks of stars. You'd long since had to give up sleeping on the ground. The earth was soft and loamy, easy to sink into, but even with a barrier between you and the dirt you could not shake the sensation of microscopic legs crawling over your skin, overtaking you. Filtering through the fronds, ever so gradually swallowing you, like a warm dark salivating mouth dissolving a morsel on its tongue.

You woke to nightmare, jolted awake with the sensation of falling down a pit. They were standing over you, an indistinct number of them, blurred like fingers hovering inches from your face. You could make out nothing of them in the dark. An awful stillness; a coffin lid weighing down on you like eyes. You screamed. There was rushing air, the sound of wings, and then you were alone again, set adrift in the darkness with only the pitons of your heartbeat to act as anchor. The moon of your father's eye hung overhead, full and clouded. From your vantage, you could see the shadows of their figures streaking across the grass until they vanished into the woods.

Your father's corpse is inhabited by vampires.

They approach in groups, shoulder to shoulder in funereal procession, waxen faces staring from rough-spun black shrouds. In the days that follow, you sleep fitfully throughout the day, sit awake by night next to the crackling heat of a bonfire, watching for their ever-so-faintly luminous pallor by the boundaries of the firelight. Their presence has upended your understanding of the world, of your place in it. You are not safe. You have never been safe. You are a child playing at survival, surrounded by stones and sticks and rusty tools, the pitiful evidence of your make-believe.

Your mind races with plans to trap them, defend against them, kill them, retracing the steps until you can feel ruts wearing into your mind. Deep dark pits papered over with leaves, open graves waiting for sunrise. Barricades hammered through with stakes. Trenches of running water. More bonfires. Burning flesh. Staggered piles of ash. The bonfire turns the night sweltering, waves of heat beating down your neck. So much of what you have built is useless. You will have to begin again.

———————

An autumnal senescence settles over your father's corpse. The leaves are changing color. Pigment bleeds from their black-veined laminae to become a clotted red at first, imperceptible but for a smeary haze of sunlight through the canopy. The early morning air brushes your nape with clammy fingers. The foliage grows anemic, paler still, color retreating beneath the surface. Dead grass crumples beneath your footsteps into dustings of dried blood.

The landscape blossoms into a motley of streaky reds, scabbed umbers, fading crepuscular blues. The grounds are spotted with rosacea. Raspberries blister up from the sunken earth, already oozing and overripe. You can pick them by the handful, juice dripping down your chin and fingers, staining your teeth and palms.

You trek deeper into the interior of your father's corpse, your keen eye finding traces of habitation hitherto unnoticed. The wild clusters of wheat and corn, now evidence of field and farmland before yours, gone wild perhaps, or maintained only sporadically. A sinkhole that might be the mouth of a well. Cairns collapsed into mounds of dirt and stone, spaced together to suggest settlements, nigh indistinguishable from the rock-strewn landscape. You sweep aside the wet leaves to press a palm against the graves, imagining their inhabitants shifting beneath their blanket of dirt, monstrous and blind, dreaming of moonrise. The raspberries you fail to eat rot from the branch, sickly-sweet spatters of pulp clotting the soil. Everything is dead, or dying. Roots swell beneath the skin, darkening and contused, bloated with the dregs of dying leaves.

You thrust red-stained hands into the dark loam and unearth distended yams, deep black and purple potatoes, twisted masses of unrecognizable tubers. Everything is distilling to its lowest point. The earth calls out for harvest. Perhaps the animals likewise are retreating, withdrawing into burrows of their own beneath the soil. Game seems scarce these days, or perhaps you have never quite become adept at hunting. The chill in the air raises the hairs on your skin, leaves you anxious. You work feverishly, dirt caked beneath your fingernails, between your toes, in the creases of your neck and wrists and thighs; you fall asleep tasting it. Dawn, till dusk; days, then weeks. Beneath the roots of your house, a stockpile grows: bushels of yams and teratomata and potatoes, dried ears of corn, jars and jars of congealing jelly, long flayed strips of preserved meat.

Your house has grown to accommodate your urges. A cellar, the beginnings of a tunnel painstakingly excavated into the earth, cool and dry with gently curving walls and shelves of jutting shale. You can descend into the musty solitude, lit by candles of rendered fat, and take inventory. You have built walls, simple fortifications of poles driven into the ground, logs piled high and wedged between them. Silverware juts from the gaps, warding. You have strung a roof of sailcloth across the branches to shield you from the rain, partitioned out rooms and laid walkways of planks between them. A ghost lantern hangs from your window, a dying breath of methane rescued from a swamp, shivering with pale blue fire. The silver casing of the pocket watch sits in the middle of your door, repurposed into a doorknob. The vampires come in the night and sit under your window and barter for your blood, and the silver burns whorls into their palms.

Apart from that, they have proven peaceable enough. It was on the sixth day that they finally approached you, one of them nudged forward, palms outstretched like blind probing feelers. You did not trust them. You had no choice but to trust them. They seemed hesitant, and almost deferential to you, shuffling backwards to accommodate your gaze. You communicated through pantomime at first: tensed postures and darting eyes, small placating gestures. A spear raised up. Shadows dancing by the firelight. A mouth unhinged to display fangs. Eyes glinting in the darkness; the turning of a hand palm-up, the wrist exposed. The deliberate withdrawal and procession back into the shadows. The long minutes of silence. The sinking terror and relief of knowing you were, at least for the moment, completely and utterly alone.

From your daylight exploration of the cairns you have seen the progress of their once-abandoned fields, new furrows hewn, tender shoots sprouting from the soil. Scattered amidst the graves you have found discarded shavings of stone, shards of pottery, figurines of twisted rag and twig; no sign of weapons. They are farmers. They do not hunt. Your presence here unnerves them. They are overly accommodating, unfamiliar with the roles of predator and parasite. They are unused to wanting to feed on someone, and the sudden rush of desire they experience around you leaves them trembling. Every bird and beast and daemon on your father's corpse is a scavenger, vampiric and bloodless, used to living off the soil. You are the only thing on your father's corpse that bleeds.

You hang the ghostlight in your window to signal for them to approach, and talk well into the night from the safety of your bedroom. You sit within the shivery circle of light and listen to the sounds of their flesh burning against the silver, the hisses and quiet exultations of pain. Come dawn you retrieve the empty vials left on your doorstep, and you prick your fingers and measure out your blood, drop by precious drop.

Your blood is as a drug to them, a ley line drawn from wrist to throat to heart, its gleam anointing their lips or used in hallucinogenic rituals. They trade freely for it, baskets of goods paraded beneath your window, wheedling in their sibilant tongue. A vial buys you a newly crafted tool, a week's worth of grain, a night of labor. You have spent nights awake, supervising, watching pale flocks of hands lay beams across rafters, raise wooden frames into place. They work in near silence, uncomplaining, the walls rising as if by pantomime.

Your house is furnished with conveniences you could have never imagined for yourself, crafts refined beyond your fumbling attempts at trial and error. Blankets and serapes of intricate patterning, soft and tufted, with a faint gamey scent when you bury your nose in their warmth. What beasts they may herd are unknown to you—all the game you have seen thus far are hairless, callow striplings—but some nights you imagine you see the shadow of clouds rolling across the blind expanse, for a moment engulfing the heath in a denser, deeper dark. Their territory is unmapped; their cairns go deeper than you have discovered. Your shelves are laden with bowls and jars tinted green with verdigris, knives and awls of alloyed copper, rows and rows of vials of clear glass.

They have taught you their songs and gifted you with little effigies of rag and twig and glass beads, either toys or things of ritual. They are generous with their offerings. Come summer they will be gone again, though to where they will not tell you. There is a wistful acceptance on their lips as they fall silent, as if imagining a faint and distant shore. Once the heat starts to rise, the swelter of your father's corpse will become inhospitable for their pallid constitutions, and they will by necessity take their leave of you, their abandoned villages sinking back into obscurity. You will be alone again, hermitic and wild. All will be as it was before.

———

You stand on your doorstep hefting your new ax, the counterweight of the ax-head cast in alloyed copper, metal burnished into fading sunset. The handle sweeps low, gently curving like a spine. Your new tools sing. You have refined your own technique through study and imitation—the same principles applied to a hoe, a scythe, a pick—but have yet to match the artisans at their craft. The polished wood of the ax handle is rippled black, smooth and sleek as a coffin lid. Cold to the touch, no matter how long your hand has gripped it. You study the shapes of trees littering your territory, the slouching angle of their trunks, the inclination of their branches. You pace out the edges of a new clearing, one vaster still, carving the overgrowth of forest back.

The ax bites down. The wood flinches and gives way. A gash of splintered teeth becomes a scream. You swing again,

again, again, the weight of a fresh shovelful of dirt thudding through your arms and chest with each stroke. The tree shudders, sways, stolidness sublimating into momentum. You used to have dreams of slitting your wrists open and letting the vampires swarm over you, raising you up and upturning their mouths to catch the falling blood. You could not have built your house without them. The world tilts on its axis, topples. Your veins bleeding dry until they had sold you every last thing they owned.

You no longer trade your blood with them. You like to think you're past that now. Self-sufficient.

There is an interior to your father's corpse still left unexplored. The great black tangle of the Wilds, inhabited by things howling and open-mouthed and chthonic. Creatures shriek in the branches and make abortive attempts at flight, trying vainly to escape the strangling ceiling of branches that snares their wings and keeps them trapped. The vampires venture into the Wilds freely, and bring back tales of the World Tree, fallen, its trunk sloughing into rot. Once it touched the sky, they say, branches extending into undiscovered worlds, but now it is dead and shrunken and takes merely a day to circumnavigate. They bring back scrapings of its bark and sap to use as fertilizer, as it bears the rot of a dozen worlds and can make anything grow. It stinks horribly, the smell clinging to the inside of your nose and throat, and you refuse to use it. Of the beasts within they say little. You believe it is because the vampires refuse to speak ill of their kin.

Your father's corpse used to be a vibrant jungle once, and the air rose humid off the sea, but now the rivers and oceans are cooling, succumbing to gravity. Everything trickles down to the depths, carrying the refuse of the world with it. The ocean is a deep purplish blue and it chills your flesh to touch it, and the winds bring in the taste of salt. There is a melancholy to the world out by the sea. The wind drops low and sighs. It tells you everything that you have built will fall away.

There is the insurmountable peak of your father's skull, so massive that it drags the clouds from the sky, keeps the moon and sun in its orbit. It is hollow, you believe, lifeless, and only the slow collapse of its walls accounts for the growl of thunder. And yet it stands prominent in the sky, judging everything beneath it, calling for you to conquer it. Deep beneath the earth are deposits you have yet to mine, pitted outcroppings protruding from the hillsides as the dirt erodes. Erosion grinds away implacably over months, thunders past in seconds. There is a storm, a flood, a tremor, and the next day you find exposed ridges of feldspar and pumice, porous and reeking and still warm to the touch, a roiling heat bubbling up from the damp soil. You live in the middle of the world, surrounded by hell above you and hell below. Your father is dead, and decaying, and still he contains multitudes. Still he contains you in your entirety.

For a while you lived in a tree, the biggest and tallest one you could find, so as to better survey the world beneath you. You rigged a primitive pulley system, clambering up into the tree and looping a rope over branches, suspending planks and then pulling them up after you. You had no idea how complex it was to make a treehouse, but you managed it in the end, a precarious arrangement of walkways and ramps and ladders and canvas tenting. Later, you hollowed out the tree itself, tunneled down past its roots to find the abandoned caverns beneath. The shale was fragile as chalk, and you widened the tunnels at your leisure, listening to the walls shift around you. New walls rose. Rafters replaced sailcloth. You have laid down stones to solidify your foundation, churning together clay and lime.

Your house has grown. It's become respectable. Its walls are gleaming and black, its perimeter ringed with silver and thorns. Your expeditions have produced uncapped reservoirs of sebum and bitumen: oil to feed your lanterns, pitch to varnish your walls watertight. Lanterns burn throughout the night, the pitch-black patina of your house painted with false sunrise, the boards themselves pungent with eucalyptus and garlic, a repellent primer infused into the wood. You have swept the vials from your shelves, unstrung beads to clatter alongside them, the shards of glass going white-hot and shapeless in your kiln. Light warps through the pebbled surface of your windows, the world painted through compound cataractous eyes.

You are planning a new wing to your house, expanding into further storerooms. Your cellar swells, teeming and gravid, cured meats dangling like entrails from the rafters, jars cradling skinless and unborn things. You have grown adept at butchery. Implements of bone and ivory adorn your table, serve as rasp and hook and knife and needle; all the things that puncture, rend, incise.

Your forays into the Wilds have revealed to you all variegation of new beasts: two-limbed, three-limbed, four-limbed, lurching and slavering and in advanced stages of decomposition, muscles unraveling into fraying strands. They are horrifying, suppurating mockeries of the beasts of the forest and the field. They die as easily as any other. It takes a week's worth of soaking to get the stench out of the fleece, a putrescent bacterial film forming on the surface of the water, hungry for the next hide to be submerged. Pelts carpet your floor, serve as binding and upholstery and bedspread. Their meat is heady, almost sweet, carrying the tang of fermentation. Drippings of yellow fat hiss and sizzle on the coals of your firepit, warmth against the encroaching cold. A black plume rises from the chimney of your house, serving as warning and a sign.

You will reshape the world. You have driven back the wilderness, with ax at first, and then with fire. Dry leaves catch like tinder. Days of burning, shrieking tides of vermin driven out beneath the waves of smoke—you stand by with gunnysack and club and slaughter them by the dozens, exhume curled-up bodies still slowly cooking in the ash. Your footprints mar the gray landscape, charred remains crumbling back into loam, all fertile possibility, as if you were settling the surface of the moon. You have cauterized the earth, burned out thorn and briar by their roots. The budding grafts of your farmstead span to the horizon. You have slit your palms open on thorns, pissed markings onto your boundaries, and churned earth into clay. You have pressed clay into brick, hardened brick in fire. You have scavenged together lumps of cold iron, turning their scarred surface over in your hands, imagining molten plumules of radiance emerging from the seedbed of your forge, a harvest sheathed anew in iron.

You have begun the work of reclamation, carving canals into the earth and damming off ponds, watching your stock of sea life grow. Beds of oysters slowly suffocate in brackish furrows, translucent eels make sluggish loops in their shallow pools. You have hunted down the reclusive beasts of the forests and leashed them to your cart and butchered and bred them for meat. You have witnessed birth, gangling bodies slick with amniotic fluid, squeezing your arm past the birth canal to un-hook hoof from hipbone. A great wailing rupture, a cold snout snuffling mucus into your palm. The babes have imprinted on your scent. The harvest has been seeded with your blood and fluids. The fish lap up your blood, and it circulates dark in their translucent frames, clotting and becoming something substantial. New shoots spring from the earth. You are grow-ing your own monsters.

You will stand atop the peak of the world, atop your father's skull, and look down and claim all that you survey. The wind will roar with your voice, the ground will beat with your pulse. You will look upon your own corpse, and delight at the recog-nition. On that day, your house will be complete.

Poetry

THE BREEZE & THE BLACK DOOR

Mack W. Mani

I heard some movement at my front door
but it was just a storm.

Drank my beer over the sink
so I didn't stain my shirt anymore.

Fixed the leak
and found a place on the floor.

Wife's been leaving the back door unlocked.

Not every night,
but enough to raise the question.

She bought some paint and a brush home
from Benny's Department Store.

Had me paint that old back door
as black as a raven.

So I stripped myself to the waist
to feel the Halloween breeze
and did as she pleased.

I heard her unlock it
last night in her sleep.

There's nothing out there beyond the fence
except the old house and the woods.

Nothing to be scared of, I guess.

But some mornings she sits
perched over her coffee
staring at the aspen,
eyes slow-rolling
over folds of barking dogwood bracken.

We used to take long walks, you know?

Down old logging roads
looking for railroad spikes and animal bones.

Once we found cloven footprints in the snow.

The kingdom of timber throne,
empty to the air
a stark, bent branch chair.

And every night before dawn
wild dogs howled across the countryside,
and we filled our cups with stray pup laughter.

Now there's a man coming at us
through the duff
out there.

How did he do it,
I wonder?

Find a way through the maze,
uncut unscathed
the come-gone scent of slapdash rain.

Sometimes it's hard not to feel
like one of her dreams.

Like dirt under her nail.

Like the evergreen Studebaker
her aunt used to drive.

She used to dream of an office in Chicago
where she could sit and watch the people go by.

Far from the farm
and the weathervane crows,
somewhere down the highway
past the hills and throes.

He'll take her there someday,
I suppose.

When I walk the path of dazzling brier,
when I retire.

Lay down my hammer
and sigh.

Find the little town upriver
where her uncle once sowed treason.

When the day retreats
and I tip my cap
to the dead-leaf days of autumn.

When she forgets even the mystery of me.

When the breeze rolls in through the black door.

Then I'll stay.
Then I'll stay.
Then I'll stay.

AUTHOR BIOS

CHARLOTTE (SEA) SUTTEE lives in the South Atlantic Rainforest in Brasil.

ALAN M. FISHER is an attorney living in Washington, D.C. He's published two novellas, *Servant of the Muses and A Pearl for Her Eyes,* under the name Brad White. He has had stories in *City in the Ice, Starship Sofa,* and *Dark Divinations.* His favorite authors include John le Carré, William Gibson, Raymond Chandler, and Neal Stephenson. When not writing, he enjoys playing board games with his wife and sons and running role-playing games for his friends.

MARISCA PICHETTE is a queer author based in Massachusetts. She has published more than three hundred pieces of short fiction and poetry, appearing in *Strange Horizons, Clarkesworld, Vastarien, The Deadlands, Fantasy Magazine, Asimov's, Nightmare Magazine,* and many others. Her poetry collection, *Rivers in Your Skin, Sirens in Your Hair,* was a finalist for the Bram Stoker and Elgin Awards. Their eco-horror novella, *Every Dark Cloud,* is out now from Ghost Orchid Press.

PHOUA LEE is a Hmong American writer and MFA Creative Writing student at California State University, Fresno. Her work has been nominated for the Pushcart Prize, Best New Poets, and Best Small Fictions, and published in *Asian American Writers' Workshop, Fractured Lit, A Velvet Giant,* and poets.org, among others.

DMITRI AKERS is an Ibaloi warrior-poet, living on an intergalactic wavelength. But he, uh, sometimes materialises on Kaurna country. His prose has appeared in *Skull & Laurel*, *Spawn 2*, and *Penumbra*. He founded a one-man research and development program to capture the elusive cryptid *thomae rugglesum Pynchonus*. Lure it with jazz and bait it with pizza. Dmitri can be hired as an editor at www.prairieandzoyd.com. His Instagram posts film photography @prairieandzoyd.

ROBIN WHEELER is a veteran writer based in the St. Louis area. Her writing has been published by Woody Guthrie Poets, *To-Go Zine*, Another Jane Pratt Thing, and a variety of anthologies, alt weekly papers, and websites. Her upcoming book, *Ribbon of Highway*, follows her journey as she chases the ghost of folk icon Woody Guthrie. When not writing, she's often on the road. Robin documents her travels at 6daysontheroad.substack.com.

JEREMY MORRIS is a writer whose work has been featured in print, TV, and documentaries. He has won a Sloan Fellowship, the McGill Theater Prize, and the Jubilee Prize. He is a graduate of McGill University and USC's Peter Stark Producing program. For five years, Jeremy worked for Robert Downey Jr.'s production company as his head of research. As an independent producer, he was drawn to stories at the intersection of folk tales, high technology, and human mortality. He was born and raised in Canada and now lives in NYC with his wife, his twin children, and their calico cat.

gray lindsey is a poet from Florida. They are pursuing an MSW at the University of Chicago, where they hope to work toward decarceration for marginalized populations. Their writing's themes cycle between spirituality, psychedelia, queerness, and working class politics. Some of their work can be found in *TEA Literary Magazine*, *Bacopa Review*, and *Unfurl, Tender Bodies*. When they're not writing, you can find them learning a new art form or petting a neighborhood cat.

JOE KOCH writes literary horror and surrealist trash. Their books include *The Wingspan of Severed Hands*, *Convulsive*, *Invaginies*, and *The Couvade*, which received a 2019 Shirley Jackson Award nomination. His short work appears in *Nightmare Magazine*, *Southwest Review*, *Vastarien*, *The Mad Butterfly's Ball*, and many others. Find Joe (he/they) online at horrorsong.blog.

ALIYA WHITELEY'S stories have been shortlisted for multiple awards. Her future-fantasy travelogue, *Three Eight One*, was published by Solaris in January 2024 and won the BSFA award for Best Novel, and her new fantasy/SF novel, *The Misheard World*, will be published in February 2026. Her short fiction has appeared in many places, most recently as a collection on the subject of transport called *Drive or Be Driven*. She lives in Sussex, UK, and blogs regularly about plants, planets, and other strange things at aliyawhiteley.uk.

SADOEUPHEMIST has been published by *Lightspeed Magazine* and has written a number of short stories across Reddit and Tumblr, one of which was the basis for the Ignatz award–winning comic *The God of Arepo*. Those older stories can still be found online.

MACK W. MANI is a Pacific Northwest based author and poet. His work has appeared in publications such as *Strange Horizons*, *The Pedestal Magazine*, and *The Rhysling Anthology*. In 2018 he won Best Screenplay at The H.P. Lovecraft Film Festival. He currently lives with his husband in Portland, Oregon.

STAFF BIOS

SEAN MARKEY publishes websites for a living and has always dreamed of starting a publishing company (about Death). He lives with his wife, Beth, and a handful of well-traveled pets, in northwest Spain.

E. CATHERINE TOBLER is a writer and editor. You might know her editing work from *Shimmer Magazine.* You might know her writing from *Clarkesworld, Lightspeed,* and *Apex Magazine.* A trebuchet and Oxford comma enthusiast, she enjoys gelato and beer in her free time. Leo sun, Taurus moon. You can find her on Bluesky @ecatherine.com.

NICASIO ANDRES REED is a writer, poet, and essayist whose work has appeared in venues such as *Shimmer, Fireside, Lightspeed,* and *Uncanny Magazine.* He's read slush for *Strange Horizons,* edited manuscripts for award-winning authors, and owns five different copies of *Moby Dick.* He lives with his family in Cavite province in the Philippines.

INKSHARK is a scandalously queer illustrator, author, and editor who lives in the rainy wilds of the Pacific Northwest. He enjoys exploring with his dogs, writing impossible things, and painting what he shouldn't. When his current meatshell begins to decay, he'd like science to put his brain into a giant killer octopus body with which he promises to be responsible and not even slightly shipwrecky. Pinky swear.

DAVID GILMORE is a writer, reader, and editor out of St. Louis, MO. His work has been featured in *The Rumpus* and at Lindenwood University, where he also received his MFA. He lives with his family and spends his free time manning a stall in the Goblin Market selling directions to various Underworlds in exchange for rumors and information on where he can find his muse.

AMANDA DOWNUM is the author of *The Necromancer Chronicles, Dreams of Shreds & Tatters,* and the World Fantasy Award–nominated collection *Still So Strange.* Not content with armchair necromancy, she is also a licensed mortician. She lives in Austin, TX, with an invisible cat. You can summon her at a crossroads at midnight on the night of a new moon, or find her on Bluesky as @stillsostrange.

LAURA BLACKWELL is a freelance copy editor and Shirley Jackson Award–winning writer. Her publications include stories in *Chiral Mad 5, Nightmare,* and the 2023 Shirley Jackson Award winner *Aseptic and Faintly Sadistic: An Anthology of Hysteria Fiction.* Visit her website—and if you like, sign up for her newsletter—at pronouncedlahra.com.

CHRISTINE M. SCOTT has been a professional graphic designer, website developer, and brand consultant for more than thirty years. She is the creative director and copublisher of Nosetouch Press and has coedited seven anthologies, including the folk horror anthology trilogy *The Fiends in the Furrows.* She is also an artist and craftsperson—several of her handcrafted items were included in *Game of Thrones: The Compendium,* printed by Chronicle Books for HBO. For a complete list of her pursuits, please visit christinemariescott.com.

FELICIA MARTÍNEZ is a writer and artist born and raised in Eastern New Mexico, though home is now the San Francisco Bay Area. She is a 2023 Dream Foundry Contest for Emerging Writers finalist, an honor she achieved with a beloved work of flash. Find her on Bluesky and Instagram as @feliciafm.

ANNIKA BARRANTI KLEIN is a freelance editor with a writing habit. Her work can be found at annikaobscura.com. She is supervised by a cat at all times.